"I'm guessing you don't still have that promise ring I gave you."

Kait found herself speechless. Why ~~was~~ she surprised? That was R~~yan~~ ~~...~~ ~~h~~ please.

The silence stre~~tched~~ head and narro~~wed~~ ask you a questi~~on~~

"Only one?"

"Oh, I've got a dozen or so more, but I'm guessing maybe it's best for both of us to take it one at a time."

"Ryan, I..."

He held up a palm. "No. A long time ago I convinced myself that you must have had a really good reason for leaving. Whatever I did, well, there's not much I can do about it now. So I'm just praying that in your own good time you'll tell me."

Their eyes met, and she glimpsed the pain in his eyes. She raised a brow, ready to hear his one question.

"Did you ever think of me?"

Kait swallowed, focused on the faded gray boards of the porch floor. "Yes."

In truth, she'd never stopped thinking about him.

Books by Tina Radcliffe

Love Inspired

The Rancher's Reunion
Oklahoma Reunion

TINA RADCLIFFE

has been dreaming and scribbling for years. Originally from Western N.Y., she left home for a tour of duty with the Army Security Agency stationed in Augsburg, Germany, and ended up in Tulsa, Oklahoma. While living in Tulsa she spent ten years as a certified oncology R.N. A former library cataloger, she now works for a large mail-order pharmacy. Tina currently resides in the foothills of Colorado where she writes heartwarming romance. You can reach her at www.tinaradcliffe.com.

Oklahoma Reunion
Tina Radcliffe

Recycling programs for this product may not exist in your area.

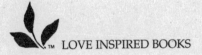 LOVE INSPIRED BOOKS

ISBN-13: 978-0-373-81580-7

OKLAHOMA REUNION

www.LoveInspiredBooks.com

Printed in U.S.A.

Behold, I am with you and will keep you wherever you go, and will bring you back to this land; for I will not leave you until I have done what I have spoken to you.
—*Genesis* 28:15

Many thanks to my sister Anne, who is my patient, long-suffering first reader and is willing to tell me what I don't want but always need to hear. Thank you to Julie Lessman and Mary Connealy for listening with two ears and one mouth. I am ever grateful for my wonderful husband, Tom, who gets me and can cook.

Thank you, K.C. Frantzen, for proofing my vet stuff and a shout-out to Michael Joseph Russo for your inspiring vet clinic stories and pictures. The iguana tail, however, I could have done without.

Thank you to Melissa Endlich and Rachel Burkot for patiently helping me dig inside myself to find the writer I can be. And a final thank-you to my wonderful agent, Meredith Bernstein, for always being positive and encouraging and for taking time from her vacation to contract this book.

Chapter One

"Unca Ryan, that mama pig has six babies." Five-year-old Faith's pudgy fingers clutched the fence surrounding the Tulsa State Fair's animal birthing pen.

Ryan Jones pushed his straw Stetson to the back of his head. "Yes, she does, darlin'," he answered.

"That's lots of brothers and sisters," Faith continued, her gaze intent upon the plump sow and her suckling brood.

Those who overheard chuckled. Ryan merely smiled, proud of his precocious niece.

When Faith finally looked up, she wriggled her button nose. "It stinks in here."

Ryan laughed. "Yeah. I guess it does." As a vet, he was accustomed to the pungent hay and animal smells, but the air in the huge livestock building had become unusually thick and dank as the number of spectators increased.

From the corner of his eye, he caught the movement of a dark-haired woman at the other end of the barnyard.

He froze, then shook his head.

Knock it off. It's been eight years, Jones. Time to stop thinking every brunette with a certain gesture or walk is Kait Field.

While he'd routinely convinced himself he was long over his first love, his stubborn heart refused to release her memory.

It didn't help that his imagination worked overtime in crowds. And this was quite a crowd.

He knelt down next to his towheaded niece. "Are you about ready for some cotton candy?"

Faith's wispy ponytail bobbed as she nodded.

"Pink or blue?" he asked.

Dimples appeared. "Pink, please."

It didn't take long to guide her through the jammed arena and back outside to the main strip of the fairgrounds.

Faith ignored the noise of the carnies vying for their attention and the loud barker at the entrance to one of the sideshows. Her short, chubby legs propelled forward on the midway, past the Ferris wheel, carousel and the sweet and greasy trailing aroma of a funnel-cake stand.

When Faith picked up her pace, Ryan reached for her hand before she got too far ahead. Not even a flamboyant clown on stilts could stop the little girl now that she had a mission.

"There." Sugar radar intact, Faith pointed to a concession stand shaded by a bright blue-and-white-striped umbrella.

"Taste good?" Ryan asked as they settled on a bench, out of the wilting heat and humidity. Early autumn in Tulsa, it was still seventy-five degrees in the shade.

Faith nodded, not wasting time on words, simply stuffing pink fluff into her mouth. When the last of the treat disappeared, she licked each finger one by one and looked up.

"I have to go to the little girls' room." She hopped off the bench and straightened her shorts and matching top. "Now," she added.

"Yes, ma'am."

Ryan stood and glanced around, spotting the nearest facility. They quickly headed over.

He narrowed his gaze, assessing those who came in and out the gray metal door. All he had to do was find a nice elderly lady or a mother with a baby to watch her inside.

"Now, please, Unca Ryan," Faith cried, reaching up to tug on his rolled-up shirtsleeve.

"I heard you, darlin'."

"Do you need some help?"

His head jerked at the sound.

That voice.

The air whooshed from his lungs as he connected with familiar dark eyes. He froze, realizing he'd just been poleaxed by the ghost of Kait Field.

"I...we..." His thoughts were as muddled as his speech.

One thing was certain. This time it wasn't his imagination. Kait *had* been in the livestock barn this morning.

Faith released a loud wail and crossed her little legs like miniature pretzels. Though Ryan heard her plea, he couldn't seem to move.

Kait, however, wasted no time. "Jenna, take the little girl into the restroom, sweetie."

"Sure." The young girl at Kait's side smiled at him before she pulled open the door and followed Faith inside. Merely a few years older than his niece, her long hair was the same rich black shade as Kait's. In fact, except for the fringe of bangs, she looked exactly like Kait.

"That's your—"

"Jenna," Kait quickly added.

He frowned, trying to piece the picture together. Kait was married and had a daughter? Regret slammed into him with the force of an Oklahoma twister.

"Your daughter is adorable, Ryan."

"Faith is my niece—Maddie's daughter."

Kait shook her head and shifted uncomfortably. When she pushed the long hair off her shoulders in a nervous gesture, he glanced at her hand, noting the light band of skin on her ring finger, evidence she'd recently removed a ring.

Hope flared and his breath tightened in his chest. The last ring he'd seen on Kait's hand was his promise ring—eight years ago.

Ryan tensed, clenching his jaw. Was she married or not?

He sure intended to find out.

"Um, well, it certainly is nice to see you," Kait finally said.

Numb and speechless, he could only stare. His world had been knocked off-kilter, and she'd just responded like they were old friends who ran into each other once a week at church.

"Come again?" Ryan bit back the slow, simmering anger deep in his gut.

"I said, it's nice to—"

"Yeah. I heard you." He jammed his hands into the pockets of his Wrangler jeans and glanced down at the ground. There was no way he could play a game of nonchalance and repartee.

No, this was too cruel, carrying on a polite

conversation while sneaking glances to see how she'd changed.

Had she changed? Not really. The woman in front of him was still tall and slim, with high cheekbones hinting at her part-Cherokee heritage. Her hair hung like a satin sheet around her shoulders—not unlike the picture he carried in his heart.

"You look good, Kait. Real good." The words slipped from his lips before he realized he'd said them.

Her face turned pink. "Thank you," she said, while fidgeting with the silver chain tucked inside her blouse. As he recalled, she used to keep her mother's wedding ring on the end of that necklace.

Kait glanced around the fairgrounds, looking anywhere to avoid the intense green eyes of Ryan Jones. What were the odds of finding this particular cowboy among all the cowboys at the Tulsa State Fair?

Yes, she'd come home to deal with the past. But she hadn't expected it would be today, her first day back in Oklahoma.

When she'd spotted Ryan, she and Jenna were walking and chatting. Suddenly there he was, giving life to the memories she'd put on a shelf eight years ago.

The same unruly golden hair peeked out from beneath his hat, and he wore a familiar uniform of a denim shirt rolled up to the elbows, faded but creased Wrangler jeans and dusty boots. Tall and lanky, there was still a sparkle in his eyes and an irreverent grin on his face.

Flustered, and with her blood beating loudly against her temples, Kait scrambled for a course of action. Her initial instinct had been to hide, but Ryan looked in need, as did the child with him. Her heart kicked in well before her brain.

Now as they stood awkwardly, waiting for the girls to come out of the restroom, she tried not to stare, but again and again her gaze returned to the tall cowboy.

"Hey, Doc, how's it going? Good to see you out having fun for a change."

Ryan's head swiveled around as he nodded a greeting to a man passing by.

"Doc?" Kait repeated the word.

"Doctor Jones. Princess says to tell you hello."

"Afternoon, Ms. Anderson." He tipped his hat to an elderly woman

"Princess?" Kait asked.

"Red tabby Persian."

"Excuse me?" Confused, she cocked her head.

"I'm a vet, Kait. I told you I was going to go to vet school."

"Your mother said you were going to law school."

He frowned, and his lips became a thin line. "And you believed everything my mother told you?"

She looked away, shaken by the harsh reply.

"Kait."

Slowly she glanced back to Ryan.

"I…" He inhaled then released a breath of air through pursed lips. "I'm sorry."

Kait gave a short nod of acknowledgment. He was angry, and she supposed he had every right to be—more than he realized, in fact.

"Is this the first time you've been back since—"

"Yes," she quickly interjected. "I have to empty out the old house before it goes on the market."

"You're selling the house? Your father…"

"My father left the house to me."

Ryan flinched. "Seems I'm always shoving my boots in my mouth. I heard he was in and out of the V.A. hospital for treatment. But I didn't realize." He cleared his throat. "When?"

Kait swallowed and stared straight ahead as she struggled to say the words without emotion. "Six weeks ago."

"I'm so sorry for your loss."

"Thank you."

"Gotta be tough," Ryan murmured.

She lifted her chin. "Time passes. Things change."

"There's an understatement." He took off his Stetson and put it back on his head. "How long will you be in town?"

"Long enough to tie up a few loose ends."

"Loose ends, huh?" A flash of pain appeared in his eyes before he quickly lowered his gaze. "So you weren't going to even stop by and see me?"

She took a deep breath at the accusation.

What could she possibly say? *Yes, Ryan. You're the reason I'm here. The reason we're here. I'd like to introduce you to your daughter.*

Instead, she barely mumbled out an inadequate response. "I did plan to see you."

Silence separated them. The same silence that had once been a comforting bond between two friends was now an insurmountable wall.

Ryan shuffled his boots on the cement. "Heard you moved East. Buffalo, right?"

"Philly." She pulled open the restroom door. "Jenna, are you coming?"

"We're washing our hands."

"Maybe we could get together later, for coffee?" He suggested.

"Discuss old times?" The last thing she wanted was to discuss old times. There was nothing to be gained from reminiscing. Moving forward was her only hope.

"Yeah. Why not?"

"We were kids, Ryan."

"Is that all we were?" he returned, with unexpected bitterness.

"A lot has happened in eight years," Kait whispered.

"Yeah, it has, and it seems I missed it all, didn't I?"

Her heart lurched. When she looked up, their eyes connected and held for a long moment.

"Kait, you left me a note. *A note.*" The words fairly exploded from his lips. He stood grim and angry, clenching and unclenching his hands.

As she opened her mouth to speak, a giggling Jenna and Faith burst out of the restroom.

Faith's little fingers curled into the palm of his big hand. When she smiled up at her uncle, the tension in Ryan's body slipped away.

Kait melted at the tender smile he gave the child beside him. Finally his gaze returned to her, and his control was back in place. "Thanks for helping me out here."

"No problem." She placed an arm around her daughter's shoulder. "We…we should be going."

"Sure." He gave a quick nod. "But I meant it

about getting together sometime. Seems to me we have unfinished business."

She bit her lip and shook her head. "Yes. Yes, you're right. We do need to talk."

Ryan stood still for a moment, as though surprised at her sudden acquiescence.

"Ryan, I really did plan to see you."

"I want to believe that." He slowly nodded. "Where are you staying?"

"Out in Granby, at the old house."

"Have you got a phone?"

"I have a cell." Digging in her purse, she pulled out a piece of paper and a pen and wrote the number for him.

When he took the paper, their fingers brushed. Kait stilled for a brief second before pulling away quickly.

"I'll give you a call."

"Okay." She looked to the child by her side.

Jenna stared curiously at Kait and then at the tall cowboy.

"Hey, there. I'm Ryan Jones. This young lady is my niece, Faith."

Faith released a squeal of childish delight at being included in the conversation, while Jenna hesitantly accepted the hand Ryan offered.

Jenna's soft-spoken words as she leaned toward Kait were loud enough that Ryan could hear. "Momma, is he—"

"We'll talk about it later, sweetie." Kait cut off the question and turned to leave.

"Kait."

She glanced over her shoulder at Ryan, her emotions whirling.

"I'm glad you're back."

"He's my daddy?"

Kait backed up the compact car and pulled away from the curb. She sensed the bubbling anticipation in her daughter. After all, Jenna had been waiting her entire life to meet her father.

"Yes."

"Does he know he's my daddy?"

"No." Kait released the word with caution.

"How come?"

"Seat belt on?"

Jenna complied but remained undeterred. "How come, Momma?"

"I wish I could explain. For now, you just have to trust me. Everything is going to work out."

Kait spoke the words and prayed she was right.

Jenna mulled the answer for a bit. Beaming, she turned to her mother. "Faith is my cousin."

"That's right."

Without skipping a beat, Jenna continued. "Do you think he already has a family?"

"What?"

"Do you think Ryan is married? Maybe he already has a little girl. He might not want another one."

Kait glanced at Jenna's stricken expression and inhaled sharply. She reached across the seat to touch her daughter's hand. "Oh, sweetheart, any daddy would love to have a beautiful and smart girl like you for his daughter."

In truth, Kait had the same questions as Jenna, along with a million others she'd considered on the long drive from Philly to Tulsa.

Jenna sighed, a pleased smile on her seven-year-old face. "Soon I'll have lots and lots of family, won't I?"

"Yes, but remember what we talked about? We have to do this in the Lord's timing. Some people have a hard time with change. It's scary, and the last thing we want is to scare them. So until it's time, this will be our secret."

Kait chewed the inside of her cheek.

If only she hadn't run into Ryan just yet. Again and again she had replayed the possible scenarios in her mind, knowing coming home meant coming face-to-face with the past.

When she looked into Ryan's eyes and he

began to speak in that deep, smooth voice laced with a dash of Oklahoma twang, she was lost.

The years melted away.

Yes, it was still there, that feeling between them. It was far more powerful than chemistry—it was a connection.

And he was right. They did have unfinished business.

Kait turned onto 31st Street and shook her head.

Ryan was a vet.

She was no less than astounded to learn he had found the courage to stand up to his family. He'd actually bucked his mother?

Despite his claims to the opposite, she knew firsthand that opposing Elizabeth Delaney Jones simply wasn't done. Time and again Kait wished she'd had the courage to stand up to the woman eight years ago. If she had, things would be so different.

For a brief moment, the what-ifs taunted her. Anger, regret and sadness vied for control.

Kait pushed it all aside.

She was here to close the door on yesterday, to say goodbye to her father and to tell Ryan the truth.

Her hands trembled on the steering wheel. No matter what the consequences were, she had to face them. Besides, what could Ryan's mother possibly do now?

Jenna turned from the window and smiled. "This is where you grew up?"

Kait turned left and guided the car down picturesque Lewis Avenue. They were definitely taking the scenic route to Granby.

The stately residences on Lewis were a throwback to the oil-boom days, when T-town was considered the oil capital of the world. Huge trees whose leaves had begun to turn autumn shades of gold and burnt umber flagged the curbsides, shading the large old homes and expansive lawns.

"Yes. I grew up here in Tulsa, and then we moved into my grandmother's house in Granby after she died."

"How old were you when you left Oklahoma, Momma?"

"Nineteen."

"And you went on an adventure."

"I did."

"Why didn't you come back?'

"Oh, Jen. That's...*complicated.*"

Over the years, Kait had become proficient at sidestepping the issue of Jenna's paternal heritage, offering vague generalities, quickly changing the subject or gently redirecting the conversation. But the older Jenna got, the more difficult it had become to change the subject once her daughter began tenaciously delving for answers.

With the death of Kait's father six weeks ago, everything had converged, and she realized it was time for that overdue heart-to-heart with her daughter.

Ready or not, the time had come to return to the town that had shown her the door eight years ago.

"Can we stay?"

"Stay?" Kait blinked, tuning back in to her daughter's words. "Jen, Philly is our home."

"Does it have to be? Tulsa's so pretty. Why can't we live here?"

Kait inspected the passing scenery, as if seeing it for the first time through a child's eyes. "I'd forgotten how beautiful Tulsa is." She sighed. "Can we talk about this more after we get to the house?"

Jenna nodded, a half frown on her face as she glanced back out the window. She knew she was being deterred.

"Momma? Are you sad that you aren't going to marry Steven anymore."

Kait rubbed her naked ring finger. Steven would have solved all her problems. But she couldn't, wouldn't take the easy way out. It wasn't fair to Steven. She didn't love him.

"No, honey. That's all over."

"Well then, I was wondering."

"Now what, Jen?" Kait asked, distracted as she checked over her shoulder for oncoming traffic.

"When can we tell Ryan Jones he's my daddy?"

Startled by the question, Kait turned to her daughter. "Soon," she said. But was Kait ready for soon? She hoped so.

Chapter Two

"May I go outside?" Jenna asked.

Kait looked up from where she sat cross-legged on a braided rag rug in the middle of the parlor. She'd spent most of the last hour going through the paperwork from the Realtor.

"Isn't it raining?"

"I won't get wet. I'll sit on the porch and read until lunchtime." Jenna held up a well-worn paperback.

"Okay, but wait a minute." Kait closed the folder in her hands and got to her feet. She pulled Grandmother Redbird's colorful, fuzzy afghan off the huge oak-trimmed sofa that took up much of the room and wrapped it around her daughter's shoulders.

Jenna gave an excited smile as Kait opened the screen door. The clean, earthy scent of rain greeted them.

"I lo-o-ove this porch," Jenna exclaimed with a dramatic flourish.

"When I was younger, I used to sit out here and read just like you." Kait stood in the doorway and watched the moisture hit the pavement in fat, crowned droplets.

"I wish we could live here forever."

Forever was much too far down the road to think about. One step at a time was pretty much all Kait could handle right now. She had a good job with health benefits in Philly—a job that they needed.

It was not the answer Jenna wanted to hear.

Though it had been pouring since midnight, Kait wasn't about to complain. The rain tapping against the bedroom window soothed her to sleep. It was the best sleep she'd had in a very long time.

As Jenna settled into the porch swing, rocking back and forth with a rhythmic squeak, Kait closed the screen. She wandered through the parlor to pick up her pile of papers before she made her way to the kitchen.

On a rainy day in the middle of the confusion her life had become, the century-old foursquare house was a haven, the kitchen her favorite room.

Kait inhaled. With the extra moisture in the air, it was possible to smell traces of the past—a hint of yeast and cornmeal mixed with the scent of cooking oil from the old deep fryer.

Elisi was still in this house. Kait had learned the Cherokee word for maternal grandmother when she was a child. In those days, this same house had been a magical place her parents took her to visit once a month. She never imagined she'd end up actually living here after her mother and her grandmother passed away.

Now the house was hers.

If she closed her eyes, she could easily imagine her grandmother standing at the stove stirring pepper pot soup for dinner and preparing traditional Cherokee fry bread.

Kait turned on the kitchen faucet. Water spit for several minutes before releasing a steady stream into the old porcelain sink. She filled a cast-iron pot halfway then heaved it onto the enormous white porcelain gas stove to boil.

Behind her in the pantry, a steady drip, drip, drip echoed into the air. Kait flipped on the light switch and discovered a puddle on the faded linoleum. A glance at the ceiling revealed a yellow circle where moisture dripped through and splashed to the cracked floor below.

"Great. Just great." She lifted a dented tin kettle from a peg on the wall and placed it beneath the leak. Add this to her plumbing problems in the main bathroom and her list was growing.

Fortunately the dripping hadn't come close to the shelves packed with jars of pepper jelly, fruit jams and vegetables.

She was grateful for a full pantry and a freezer stocked with home-baked casseroles. They would go a long way toward helping stretch her meager funds until the property sold. How she was going to pay the rent on the apartment back in Philly and manage the repairs on this house would be her next challenge.

Kait laughed. Life was never boring.

As she began to peel carrots for her and Jenna's own pepper pot soup, her cell phone began to ring. The number was all too familiar, and Kait couldn't hold back a smile.

Molly Springer.

"Kaitey-girl, you're back."

"Oh, Molly, it's so good to hear your voice."

"How are you doing? How was the drive?"

"Not bad. Jenna talked for twelve hours straight. That'll keep anyone alert."

Molly laughed. "Good. Are you settled in?"

"Getting there. There's a lot to do around here. My father apparently hadn't done any repairs since my mother was alive."

"I'll help. I have plenty of grandchildren who can give you a hand. No worries."

"You've already done so much. Thank you for filling the pantry and the refrigerator and for getting the electricity turned on for us."

"My pleasure."

Kait could almost see Molly's contagious smile.

"So how are *you* doing, Kait?"

"Overwhelmed but okay."

"It can't be easy coming home to all these memories."

Kait looked through the kitchen to the front door. Her very last memory of home was her father demanding she get out.

She released a shaky breath. "I'm a coward, Molly. I haven't even been able to open his bedroom door yet."

"All in good time."

"But I wasn't there for him."

Molly made a scoffing noise. "The man shut you *and* your baby out. Remember? Because if you don't, I surely do."

"Why do I always think I should have found a way in?"

"*Please.* Jack Field was bitter to the end. He refused a memorial service just to be stubborn."

"I know you're right, Molly. At least my head knows that, but…"

"But nothing. No condemnation. That is not what the good Lord wants."

Kait took a deep breath.

"Now then, when do I get to see your little girl?" Excitement laced Molly's words.

"She's not so little, Molly. She's grown since you visited us."

"Have you told Ryan yet?"

Silent, Kait stared at the bubbles rising and sinking in the cast-iron pot.

"You have to tell him. His mother's threats can't touch you anymore."

"I know. And I will." Kait exhaled. "*I will.* That's why I'm here. Finding a segue in a conversation to tell a man he has a child—well, that's not going to be easy."

"None of this is easy. But you did the right thing. You kept your baby. Now give your daughter a family. It's time."

Kait nodded, though Molly couldn't see the gesture.

"Oh, and I have the youngest grandkids here for fall break. Does Jenna want to run around with us, maybe later this week? Go to the zoo?"

"I'm sure she'd love to," Kait said.

"How long will you be here?"

"I only have over three weeks of vacation time accumulated."

"Oh, that will never do," Molly admonished. "We're going to talk about that."

Kait was still laughing when she said good-bye and put down the phone.

"Look what I found, Momma."

Kait turned. Jenna stood in the doorway holding a drenched gray tabby against her sweatshirt. "Where did you find a kitten?"

"Under the porch."

Kait moved to her daughter and gently pushed back Jenna's wet bangs. "Jen, you're almost as soaked as this poor little kitty."

"I was sitting out there reading and I heard her cry. It took me forever to get her to come close enough to pull her out."

"She's bleeding." Kait wiped her hands on her jeans and inspected the animal's torn ear. "Poor little thing must have been hiding from her attacker."

"Can we keep her?"

Moistening a kitchen towel, Kait gently applied a corner of fabric to the animal's ear. She grabbed another towel to wrap around the kitten. "Jen, why don't you change into dry clothes?"

"But can we keep her?"

Easing the shivering ball of fur into her arms, Kait looked at her daughter. "She might belong to someone."

"I can put up signs. If no one claims her, then we can keep her, right, Momma?"

Kait hesitated.

"Please?"

"Maybe." Maybe? Had she really said *maybe?* That was as good as a yes to her daughter.

Jenna's face glowed.

How could she deny this one request? They'd lived in a tiny apartment without so much as a goldfish all Jenna's life. Kait didn't have the heart to refuse a simple thing like a stray kitten. For once, she wouldn't be practical and hoped it wouldn't become a habit. She'd worry about how they were going to pay for the pet deposit at their apartment back home later.

"Do you think she's hungry?"

"Honey, go change. We're going to have to get this baby to a vet. Right away. Then we can stop and get cat food."

"Ryan is a vet. I heard him say so."

Yes. He was a vet. Kait slowly inhaled and exhaled. Why was it that she had only been back in Granby a few days and circumstances kept conspiring to put her and Jenna in the path of Ryan Jones?

"Momma?"

"Go change, and I'll get directions."

Oklahoma State University College of Veterinary Medicine. Kait inspected the framed certificates on the wall. She smiled, so very proud that Ryan had gone after his dreams.

An unexpected lump of sadness welled in her chest. She'd hadn't been there to share that journey.

Next to his certificate was that of a Lucas Hammond. So there were two vets at the clinic? That was a good thing since it was so busy. She'd watched no less than half a dozen small animals and their owners come in and out of the front door since she arrived.

Kait checked her watch. That had been quite a while ago.

She approached the counter. "Excuse me?"

The receptionist arched her penciled brows while twisting a strand of fuchsia hair around a finger but didn't put down the cell phone attached to her ear.

"How much longer do you think it will be?"

"That's hard to say. Dr. Jones is booked solid, and you didn't have an appointment."

Kait bit her lip at the accusation but decided against pointing out that the sign outside said walk-ins were welcome. "What about Doctor Hammond?"

"Who?"

"Doctor…never mind. Perhaps you can give me directions to another clinic?"

The door behind the receptionist opened, and Ryan appeared. Head down, broad shoulders slumped, he shoved a stethoscope into his lab-coat pocket and ran a hand through his hair as he checked a ledger on the counter. His guard was down, and Kait was taken aback by the fatigue and something else—discouragement perhaps—that she saw in his stance.

Ryan rarely showed any emotion, instead putting on his happy-go-lucky face for the world. She knew he must have a lot on his mind. Her heart ached, and for a moment she simply stared. How simple it would be to reach out and smooth the worry lines from his brow and give him a hug of encouragement.

With a small sigh, she turned her face away. Nothing was simple anymore.

"*Kait?* What are you doing here?"

She swung back at his voice.

When he offered a tentative smile, she froze for a moment. He so reminded her of Jenna.

Any trace of fatigue or stress had disappeared, and his smile, however wary, wrapped itself around her. Suddenly she was glad Jenna had convinced her to come to his clinic.

Kait pointed across the room to where Jenna held the kitten; both were mesmerized by the huge tropical fish tank in the corner.

"You have a kitten."

"Jenna found her. It looks like she was in a tussle."

"Who? Jenna or the cat?"

Kait swallowed a laugh at his dry humor. "The cat."

"Ah." He crossed the room. "Hey, Jenna. Good to see you again."

She turned at his voice, her face brightening. "My kitty was in a fight."

He leaned closer to inspect the kitten and then looked up at Kait. "How long have you been here?"

"About an hour," she replied.

"An *hour?*" Ryan glanced at the receptionist who kept chatting on her cell, oblivious to the note of disapproval in his voice. "I'm sorry. I can tell you that *won't* happen again." He shook his head. "Let's go back to an exam room."

Jenna looked around the small room, her interest focused on the black-and-white framed photographs on the wall. "Oh, wow. This is so cool."

"They're all my patients."

"Even that one?" Jenna pointed to a photo of a lizard sunning on a rock.

"Especially that one. That's my lizard, Roscoe."

"You really have a lizard?"

"Absolutely."

"I love animals," Jenna said.

"So do I," he responded.

"Do you like kids, too?"

Ryan chuckled, not the least bothered by the random question from Jenna. He relaxed, open and unguarded as he conversed with the seven-year-old. "Yes. I like kids, too."

"Do you have any?"

"Unfortunately, I don't."

Kait cleared her throat loudly. "Who took all these pictures?"

"I did."

"I didn't know you were a photographer."

Ryan raised a brow in challenge, the caution back in his eyes. "I bet there are a lot of things you don't know about me."

Regret washed over Kait, and she turned to the wall, feigning interest in the photos. "So this is your clinic? Yours and Dr. Hammond's?"

"How'd you know about Doc Hammond?"

"I saw his certificate on the wall."

"Old Doc Hammond went fishing six months ago and decided not to come back. He says he needs to keep his options open, so there is a slight possibility that either retirement or Mrs. Hammond will drive him nuts and he'll be back."

Kait smiled.

"Why don't you set the kitten on the table, Jenna?"

Ryan donned gloves and began to stroke the animal. "Pretty little thing, isn't she?" He skillfully examined the kitten from head to toe, finally assessing her teeth. Then he pulled out the stethoscope.

"Is she okay?" Jenna asked.

"She's going to be just fine. This little baby is about eight months old. A little underweight. But your stray is definitely a girl."

Jenna turned to Kait with a delighted grin on her face. "I was right. She's a girl."

Ryan reached for a small machine on the counter. Holding it in his hand, he slowly wanded the device over the cat's entire body. "I don't see any microchip, so I'm guessing she isn't spayed either."

"What's spayed?" Jenna's voice became concerned.

"We do surgery on animals so they don't have babies. Cats can have a lot of kittens in their lifetime. That's dozens of homeless, hungry cats."

"Will it hurt?"

"A little, but I'll let her stay here overnight. Chris, my technician, will check on her. We'll take very good care of your little one."

Ryan grabbed a pump bottle, saturated a few cotton balls and began to clean the kitten's ear.

"She's wiggling!" Jenna exclaimed with concern.

Kait reached over to help hold the animal tighter just as Ryan did. His hand covered hers.

Their eyes held.

"Sorry," Kait murmured. Embarrassed, she slipped her hand away.

Ryan lowered his gaze. "Well, Jenna, looks like the wound isn't too bad. Probably another cat. I'll give her antibiotics and put ointment on the ear."

Reaching to the counter, he grabbed several long cotton-tipped swabs and checked her ears.

"Does she get shots?"

"Yes, a few. Then you'll bring her back in a few weeks for another shot, and we'll test her to make sure she didn't pick up a virus from the bite."

Jenna nodded as Kait began to nervously tally the cost of today's visit.

Ryan handed the kitten back to Jenna. "Here you go. Are you ready to be a parent?"

Jenna's smile widened, and she nodded.

"Well then, congratulations."

He pulled off his gloves and washed his hands. "Tell you what. You show your kitty the fish tank while your mother and I take care of the paperwork."

Kait followed Ryan to the front desk where he opened a chart. She noted the strong, mature line of his jaw and the five o'clock shadow on face. In the crisp white lab coat worn over navy scrubs he looked vastly different from the rough-and-tumble carefree cowboy she had known. Ryan had become a man in the years since she'd seen him. Another unexpected pang of regret struck Kait.

"Do you still rodeo?" The question popped out before she realized she'd spoken aloud.

"What?" He looked up, brows knit.

"Rodeo."

The corners of his lips twitched, and his green eyes flashed as he leaned against the counter. "Ah, rodeo. Don't I wish? Lately my horse has become a pasture ornament, and my saddle doesn't even know my name."

His gaze wandered to Jenna, and he gave a puzzled frown before turning back to the chart, his professional mask back in place. "We'll do the surgery late tomorrow afternoon. Is that okay with you?"

She nodded.

"If it's more convenient, you can just leave the kitten here, and I'll drop her off when she's ready to come home."

"Oh, I don't want to bother you with—"

"It would be my pleasure. Let me do this for your daughter."

Your daughter.

Kait inhaled sharply at the words.

"All right. Thank you." She glanced down at Ryan's scribbles and cleared her throat. "How much do you think this is going to cost?"

"There's no charge."

She blinked. "Of course there's a charge. You examined her, treated her ear, gave her shots and she's going to have surgery."

"There's no charge." His lips became a firm line, and his taut stance brooked no discussion. "Kait, I've never stopped being your friend, even if you don't believe that. You're like family. And I don't charge family."

Speechless, she searched the depths of his gaze.

"But," he continued, "we have to talk."

She took a ragged breath. "Maybe you could stop by the house? I mean, well, I don't know your schedule or anything." Kait looked pointedly at his left hand.

"Not married, if that's what you're asking." His expression softened a fraction. "Who'd have a guy who lives at the clinic 24/7, and when he does make it home, he sleeps with two cats and a hundred-pound mutt?"

Kait resisted the very strong urge to respond. Instead, she fiddled with the chain at her neck, struggling for nonchalance.

Ryan raised his brows in question. "And you, Kait?"

"Me?"

"No ring?"

"I'm not married." She quickly glanced over at Jenna and moved the conversation along. "We have an appointment later today. But Jenna goes to bed at nine. Maybe…"

"After nine, then. I'll be by," Ryan said.

Kait swallowed, silently praying she had the courage for what was about to unfold.

Chapter Three

Ryan pushed open the door to the clinic's back room and headed to the sink.

"Hey there, Doc. What's got you looking like an agitated barnyard rooster?"

He leveled Chris LaFarge, his vet tech, a glance. "Excuse me?"

"Come on. No use denying it. You've been cranky all day. Will Sullivan pull another one on you?"

Scrubbing his hands, Ryan narrowed his gaze. He couldn't help comparing people to animals. Short and stocky with thick brown hair and a flat nose, Chris, the full-time vet tech, had always been a tenacious bulldog in Ryan's mind.

"I was hoping your attitude might improve so we could discuss all this overtime."

"You have a problem making money?"

"Naw, I like taking your money, Doc, but I've been thinking." Chris tore off a fresh plastic bag for the trash bin.

"I'm in trouble now." Ryan reached for a paper towel and dried his hands and forearms. He stepped back from the stainless-steel sink to stop the water from flowing.

"It's time you hired more help around here. Since Doc Hammond retired, it's only getting busier and busier."

"I'm not complaining, am I?" Ryan asked.

"No, but you don't have a life, either." He sprayed the counters with disinfectant and wiped them down, then glanced up. "Why, I think you'd even work Sundays if Pastor Jameson hadn't finally lassoed you into ushering at first service."

If Ryan thought his friend was done railing on him, he was wrong. Chris just kept talking, all the while efficiently restoring the counters and supply cupboards to order.

"You're going to have to let go of the past, Doc."

"What?" Ryan's head jerked up at the comment.

"I've heard the stories."

"Are you kidding me? What stories?"

"Something about a broken engagement and your true love running off."

Ryan groaned loudly. "Sounds like the lyrics to a bad country song. Where do you get this stuff?"

"Will Sullivan, I expect."

"Sullivan again? He's feeding you a load of cow pies."

"You telling me none of it's true?" Chris scratched his head.

"There might be a grain of truth buried somewhere in that malarkey but not enough to be recognizable."

"You weren't jilted at the altar?"

"No."

"She didn't run off in her graduation cap and gown?"

"No."

"Hmm."

Ryan leaned back, enjoying the fact that for once Chris was at a loss for words. It didn't last long.

"All the same, how many times have Joanie and I tried to get you over for dinner?"

There was no point responding. They both knew that if it was merely a home-cooked meal he'd been invited to, Ryan would have probably shown up more often than not. Generally, however, what appeared to be an innocent invite to supper was actually a clever match-making scheme.

"And here's the other thing, Doc."

"The other thing?"

Chris nodded and motioned to the front room. "You're going to have to do something about that sorry excuse out there answering phones." He shook his head. "Trouble with you is you only see the good in folks. That's why you haven't noticed she spends most of her day talking to her boyfriend and polishing her nails. You need someone who can handle billing and vendors. Not just a warm body who occasionally picks up the phone."

This time Ryan paused at Chris's words. He frowned and remembered Kait and Jenna's visit. Ryan liked to think he was focused. Generally, however, it was simply tunnel vision. While he loved to work with animals, and he liked people, he wasn't real good at the business end of things at the clinic. And Doc Hammond's sudden retirement also meant he'd taken Mrs. Hammond, their one-woman office staff, with him.

"Okay. Let me think on this a bit."

As much as he hated to purposely hand Chris a free ride to another "I told you so," the vet tech was right.

"While you're at it, maybe you could start thinking about dating and settling down."

"Whoa. Why does a conversation with you

have more ups and downs than a bull straight out of the shoot? Mind telling me what dating has to do with the conversation?"

"Simple. Make some changes at the clinic and you'll have time to court a woman. Why, I bet you don't even have a date for Will Sullivan's wedding."

"I'm the best man. I thought all I had to do is show up and make a speech."

"Are you hearing anything I'm saying?"

"I don't remember you telling me that particular piece of information."

A date for a wedding? Who knew? Ryan ran a hand through his hair. While Chris's logic was skewed, Ryan had to admit it had occurred to him on odd occasions that he just might indeed be running out of time. After all, he sure didn't want to find himself alone in his dotage, with only a mismatched menagerie of pets for company. He loved kids and wouldn't mind a few of his own. A daughter like his niece Faith, or…

An image of a dark-haired little girl flashed through his mind.

Chances were he had already run out of time.

Kait dried her hands on a towel and leaned against the screen door looking out at the front yard. The huge sugar maple near the street was barren of leaves, the naked branches dead and the bark peeling. It would have to be cut down which meant one more problem to solve, one more thing to do and much too much to think about.

"Oh, Lord." She closed her eyes for a moment and prayed. "Right now I ask for wisdom and guidance as I prepare to talk to Ryan and make decisions for the future. Amen."

When she opened her eyes, the first thing she saw was an ancient, mud-colored pickup coming round the corner. The Ford's aged muffler vibrated loudly in the silence of the evening.

Illuminated by the glow of the street lamp, she could see every last rusted dent in the old truck. The rear bumper was gone, and the front bumper looked like it would be tempted to fall off with very little encouragement.

When the pickup stopped across the street, she realized the driver was Ryan.

Obviously he could afford a new vehicle yet he chose one with more dents than not. What did that say about him? Perhaps this was Ryan's way of rebelling against his parents' affluence.

He hung his head for a minute then looked up at the house before turning off the engine.

Slipping out the screen door, Kait ran a quick finger under her eyes and smoothed back her ponytail. She walked to the rail.

Ryan's gaze swept the yard before he made his way to the front steps. His hands were shoved in the front pockets of his worn jeans as he stood, one boot on the rough cement of the sidewalk and one on the porch steps. The blue cotton shirt he wore was unbuttoned; with the sleeves rolled up, it hung loose over a navy T-shirt that stretched across a broad, muscular chest.

Kait swallowed, and averted her eyes. Ryan was always bigger than life—clearly the stuff women's dreams were made of.

She frowned. This had to stop. There was no time for dreams in her life.

"When you first moved to Granby, I used to drive by your house on a regular basis."

The simple statement surprised her. His face revealed nothing.

"I never saw you," she said.

"Apparently I was better at being undetected back then."

Kait bit her lip then murmured, "Perhaps you just need a new muffler."

"Could be." Undeterred, Ryan continued. "I used to park over there under the branches of that huge maple and just stare at your house for hours, trying to figure out which window was yours and hoping you'd come out." He shook his head.

Apparently a response was not required. Ryan simply stared ahead as though thinking.

That was a good thing, as Kait didn't know what to say. Bringing up memories was way too dangerous. She couldn't go back. All her energy was focused on today.

She wrapped her arms around herself and looked at the front yard. "The maple's dead now."

Ryan moved up a step, and leaned against a porch column. He glanced over at the tree. "You sure? I saw a few healthy branches."

"Not enough to save the tree."

"All that tree needs is a good pruning and a little TLC."

"That's probably more trouble than it's worth."

He shrugged. "Your call, I guess."

Silence stretched. Their gazes met. His glance moved oh so leisurely from her eyes to her lips. Kait couldn't look away.

She licked her lips and willed herself to breathe.

Ryan moved to stand mere inches from her. He'd showered since this afternoon, and she inhaled the scent of sandalwood soap and the man himself—a potent combination that left her heady. She grasped the railing for support.

"You still look like you're sixteen. Hard to believe you're someone's mother."

Kait stilled, unsure what to say.

His assessing glance moved to where her fingers remained splayed on the railing. "Divorced?"

"I was engaged." She covered her naked ring finger. "It was a mistake."

"Ah." He nodded and paused for a moment. "I'm guessing you don't still have that little promise ring I gave you."

Kait found herself speechless. Why was she surprised at his words? That was Ryan. Bold as you please. He always said what he thought.

The silence stretched until Ryan cocked his head and narrowed his eyes. "Could I just ask you a question?"

"Only one?"

"Oh, I've got a dozen or so more, but I'm guessing maybe it's best for both of us to take it one at a time."

"Ryan, I…"

He held up a palm. "No. A long time ago I convinced myself that you must have had a really good reason for leaving. Whatever I did, well, there's not much I can do about it now. So I'm just praying that in your own good time you'll tell me."

Their eyes met, and she glimpsed the pain in

his eyes once more. She raised a brow, ready to hear his one question.

"Did you ever think of me?"

Kait swallowed, wishing for a sip of sweet tea about now. She focused on the faded gray boards of the porch floor. "Yes."

In truth, she'd never stopped thinking about him. A shiver ran across her shoulders. And every time she looked at their daughter, she thought of him yet again.

"Ryan, I do want to tell you why I left. I came back to Oklahoma with that in mind, settling the past once and for all."

"Once and for all? Doesn't sound good."

"That's not what I mean."

"Momma, your phone is ringing."

Kait turned at the sound of her daughter's voice. Jenna stood at the screen.

She looked at Ryan. "Would you excuse me for a minute? I'm expecting a call from the Realtor."

"Sure." Ryan exhaled and gazed out at the yard, then glanced back at the house. Jenna stood quietly behind the screen studying him.

"Hey, Jenna."

"Hi." She watched him for a few minutes longer then quietly asked, "Is my kitten okay?"

"She is. When I left the clinic, she was curled in a little ball, sleeping."

Jenna smiled. She released a yawn and rubbed her left eye with a knuckle.

"Tired?"

She nodded. "I was going to go to bed, but my closet doors are stuck."

"Stuck?"

"They slide open, and Momma says they get off their track sometimes."

"Do you want me to take a look at them for you?"

"Yes, please."

He opened the screen and paused in the foyer. Kait was in the kitchen to his left, her back to him as she spoke to someone while eyeing a calendar on the refrigerator.

He followed Jenna upstairs, his hand on the smooth oak banister as he moved up the wide staircase of threadbare-carpeted steps to the second floor of the old house.

"That's my grandpa's room," Jenna said as they passed a five-paneled door with a crystal knob. Her voice became a hush. "We aren't allowed to go in there."

They passed another room, the door slightly ajar. "Momma's. But don't look because it's kind of messy. She's going through lots of boxes." Jenna released a frustrated sigh. "She says we can't stay."

"I see."

"This is my room. It used to be my mother's when she lived here a long, long time ago."

Not so very long ago, he mused while eyeing the simple twin bed and matching bureau. A beautiful, worn pastel quilt covered the bed. Funny, he'd known Kait since they were sixteen, and he'd never set foot inside this big old house before.

Jenna went to the closet and pushed on the door with a grunt. "It won't open."

She was right. The panels were off their track. He raised the outer panel and shoved it back into place, then the door slid open with ease. Inside, the clothes were arranged neatly on hangers.

"All fixed."

"Oh, thank you," Jenna gushed as though he'd slain dragons. She pulled a neatly folded pair of pajamas from the closet.

Ryan glanced around the room, his gaze stopping on the artwork tacked to the wall.

One large crayon drawing was of a man and a woman with a little girl in the middle. All were holding hands. For moments, he simply stared at the picture, mesmerized.

"Did you like school when you were a kid like me?" Jenna asked.

"Hmm? School?" He tore his attention from the picture. "Yeah. I liked recess best."

Jenna laughed.

Ryan looked around the room, and his glance caught a pile of books on a desk next to the bed. "Are all those schoolbooks yours?"

"Yes. I have lots of homework while we're here."

"What grade are you in?"

"Second."

Second? Why did he think Jenna was younger? Ryan frowned. Then again, Kait always did look younger than her years.

"I'm going to be eight next month."

"November?" He murmured the word.

"Uh-huh. November 25th. Momma says I'm her 'Thank You, Lord, Thanksgiving baby.'"

November.

A tremor raced through him as his mind began a panicked gallop backward.

Kait left in March eight years ago. Ryan could barely breathe as he slowly did the math. He gripped the bureau for support as his knees threatened to buckle.

"Thanksgiving baby." Ryan whispered the words aloud as he looked into Jenna's sweet face. His gaze skimmed over the dark eyes, the freckles on the bridge of her nose—a nose just like his own.

The penny fell into the slot.

Jenna was his daughter.

Chapter Four

Ryan paced back and forth on Kait's porch. He shivered as the cool evening breeze whipped past.

November. Thanksgiving baby.

What a fool he was—eight years the fool.

Conflicting emotions pummeled him. He was as thrilled as he was heartsick. Mostly he was plain ashamed.

Closing his eyes tightly, he recalled the details of the crayon drawing on Jenna's wall. It was of a family holding hands and looking out at the future.

All that that little girl wants is a family.

As if it was yesterday, he remembered one of his and Kait's last conversations so long ago. They'd discussed their plans after college— graduate program, then marriage and a family.

Ryan and Kait. Forever.

He'd kissed her tenderly beneath the soft light of this very porch before leaving her at her front door at the start of spring break.

What happened? How had it all become so convoluted?

He was a father. *Jenna's father.*

The words raced round and round in his head like a wild mustang desperate for a way out. Panic gripped him, choking his throat and clutching at his gut.

What did he know about being a father? It couldn't be nearly the same as owning a cat or a dog. If he made his beast dog Jabez neurotic, well, it scared him to think about his effect on a little girl.

He ran a hand over his pounding head and slammed his fist on the porch rail as his emotions swung wildly between despair and hysterics.

There were way too many questions and not nearly enough answers. His head ached as much as his heart.

And why had Kait kept it from him? Yeah, that was the big question. Unfamiliar rage welled up inside, threatening to erupt.

As if on cue, Kait opened the screen door and stepped onto the dimly lit porch.

"I'm sorry that took so long." She rubbed her arms with her hands. "It's gotten chilly. Do you want to come inside? I can make some tea or coffee. I have a fresh pumpkin loaf."

Kait's voice disarmed him for a moment. For all his self-righteous anger, he didn't know what to say. He couldn't even look at her. He turned away.

"Ryan? What's wrong?"

He tried to answer, but the words wouldn't obey him.

"Ryan?" she asked again. This time her voice sounded almost afraid.

Silence stretched until he couldn't hold back the question any longer. He turned from the rail as the words burst from his lips, the pain ripping him apart.

"Jenna's my daughter, isn't she?"

Kait's eyes rounded and her face paled. There was another long, painful silence. She swallowed.

"Yes."

Ryan turned back to the rail. Eyes burning, he hung his head.

"Are you going to give me a chance to explain?"

"You've had eight years to explain, Kait. Eight years." He gripped the wood tightly, blinking away emotion as he stared ahead into the settling twilight.

"Oh, Ryan," Kait whispered. *Dear Lord, this wasn't how I planned for him to find out.*

She sucked in her breath and automatically moved closer, reaching out to touch his hand. The contact started a frisson of electricity that surprised her.

Ryan jerked away. Once again, his back was to her. Several times he closed and opened his fists, finally shoving his hands into the pockets of his jeans.

"Does Jenna know I'm her father?"

"Yes."

"How can she know I'm her father when I didn't even know?"

"It was only fair to talk to Jenna before we left Philly."

"Fair," he muttered the word.

Her stomach in knots, Kait watched him pace.

He came to a sudden halt and faced her. "Why did you come back to Granby now?"

"My father died, and I hoped that maybe this was the right time to talk to you."

"Just like that."

"Yes, just like that."

Ryan was spoiling for a fight that she didn't intend to give him. She could afford the luxury of being calm. After all, she'd had a long time to think about this. She understood his anger—yes, he had every right to be mad.

Finally, he raised his head and met her gaze. Kait flinched at the raw pain in his eyes. Ryan shook his head. "Why didn't you tell me you were pregnant?" The accusation lingered in the air.

"It's not like I didn't want to tell you. The timing wasn't in our favor."

"Timing?" His eyes rounded in astonishment, and his tone became almost mocking. "You're going to try to tell me this is all about timing?"

"You were out of town for spring break sophomore year, as I recall. Some legal internship your parents had arranged in D.C."

Ryan's jaw tightened, and the muscle in his right cheek twitched. "It was a week and a half. You couldn't have waited for me? The father of your child?"

"My father kicked me out." She took a deep breath. Suddenly she had no energy to defend herself. Once again, she was convicted before she began. "I was homeless. Nineteen and pregnant with nowhere to go. I was scared, and I didn't have any options. I had to make decisions very fast."

There was more to the story. Oh, yes, much more. But Ryan certainly wasn't ready to hear everything tonight. She held back to protect him, and because deep down inside she doubted he'd believe her anyhow. What chance did her word have against Elizabeth Delaney Jones's?

For several long moments, neither of them spoke.

"Did you think I wouldn't be a good father?"

Surprised, Kait jerked back at his words. "Where did that come from? No. I hadn't even thought that far down the road, Ryan. I panicked. I didn't know what to do. I called Molly Springer, and she helped me. Molly has family in Philly. She found a place for me to stay and was there when Jenna was born."

Again Ryan's face became a twisted mask of anguish. His words were raw with pain. "I missed the birth of my daughter. Dear Lord, I've missed so much."

Aching for him, Kait considered his words, not sure how to comfort him. Suddenly he was very quiet, his face stony. His eyes moved from her ringless hand to her face. "You were going to let someone else be Jenna's father before giving me a chance."

"It wasn't…I didn't…" Her eyes pricked with emotion. "That wasn't how it was at all, Ryan."

"How was it, Kait?" He blinked and looked away. "You had years to call me. Years. That's what hurts most of all."

How could she ever explain? Time and again

she had tried to pick up the phone. With each passing day, the bridge to her past crumbled further. It was easier not to look back and to convince herself Ryan wouldn't be waiting anyhow.

"I'm sorry, Ryan. I'm so sorry."

"Sorry isn't going to cut it, Kait."

"Ryan, I—"

"No. I'm pretty sure this conversation is over." Swallowing, he straightened and glanced at his watch. "For now. It's late, and I'm functioning on an empty tank. I don't want to say something we'll both regret."

Kait nodded.

Arms crossed, Ryan met her gaze head-on. His eyes flashed cold and dark.

She shivered. She'd never seen this side of Ryan before.

"I want to get to know Jenna. I want to get to know my daughter."

He turned from her and walked slowly to his pickup, head bowed with the weight of his burden.

"That's what I want, too," Kait whispered as he drove away.

Pointing the pickup toward Tishomingo, Ryan drove. The three-and-a-half-hour trip took considerably less. It was after ten when he pulled up the long dirt-and-gravel drive and parked outside the rambling farmhouse. Twilight had long since disappeared, and a dark blanket of a country night covered everything.

The tension that held his shoulders tight and his jaw clenched finally eased. He released a deep breath and got out of the truck. Stones crunched beneath his boots as he approached the porch. The creaking of a rocking chair accompanied a chorus of cicadas.

"You know what time it is?" His grandfather's voice reached him.

Ryan glanced at his watch. "Way past your bedtime."

"Guess I must have been waiting up for you." Gramps glanced over at the truck. "You still driving that old piece of tin?"

"Gets fair mileage and keeps the women away."

Gramps laughed loud and hard.

The small porch light was enough to detail his grandfather's rhythmic motions in the chair. As usual, Gramps wore a clean white T-shirt and pair of well-worn overalls. His remaining tufts of white hair stood straight up on a shiny scalp. Nearing eighty-four, Harlan Lukas Jones never changed. Ryan thanked God for that. The man was his rock, his sanity in a crazy world.

"Everyone okay?" Gramps asked.

"Yeah."

The older man lifted a glass of lemonade to his lips. "There's more in the house. Help yourself."

"I'm good."

Gramps looped his foot around another rocker, the twin to the one he sat in, and pulled it close. "Then have a seat."

Weariness settled on Ryan as he eased into the chair and leaned against the smooth slats. "Nice weather for the first week of October."

"Bit of a breeze but nice. Frost coming soon. That'll quiet those cicadas."

Ryan nodded.

"Good chili-cooking weather, too, but I'm guessing you didn't come out here to discuss the weather or cooking. What's on your mind, son? You look like you've gone a few rounds with the devil tonight."

Ryan inhaled, steadying his emotions. "She's back."

They were silent for a while, chairs slowly moving in unison.

His grandfather gave a thoughtful shake of his head. "Time changed her?" he finally asked.

"Not really." If anything, Kait was more of everything that tugged at his heart and soul. As a woman, the emotions she stirred in him were more powerful than ever.

"What are you feeling?"

"No different." He paused, relieved at the admission. "The trouble is, I'm not sure if I'm still in love with her because that's all I know or because that's all I want to know."

"Little of both, I imagine." Gramps set his glass on the ground. "She married?"

"No." Ryan glanced down.

"Your folks never cared for Kait. You know that."

"I didn't let that stand in the way, Gramps."

"You've never gone nose to nose with your folks, either."

"I'm not a lawyer, am I?"

"This isn't like choosing veterinary medicine over law school, son. If it's change you're looking for, you're going to have to quit straddling the fence."

Ryan shook his head. He knew his grandfather was right. He rarely stood up to his parents. It was too much trouble. He'd rather find the road around an issue and quietly do things his own way.

"There's more, Gramps."

His grandfather stopped rocking.

"She brought her daughter with her."

"How old is she?"

"Seven. Almost eight."

"Are you trying to get up the nerve to tell me you're that little girl's daddy?"

Ryan blinked. "You know?"

"Not a far leap, even for an old steer like me. I always wondered when she left so sudden-like."

"I want to do the right thing, but I have to tell you, I'm reelin'." Ryan gripped the chair, his knuckles white. He released a breath, once again fighting the desire to hit something or break down in tears. Neither was an option.

Gramps reached out a gnarled hand and touched Ryan's arm. His deep blue eyes searched his grandson's. "It'll all sort itself out, son. Anger's not going to do anyone any good, so you may as well put it away and save it for something more deserving."

Ryan slowly nodded and leaned back in the chair. They rocked silently for a long time, until his grandfather spoke again. "Ha." Gramps stopped the chair and slapped his knee. "Bet this put your folks in a tizzy."

"They don't know yet."

"Ooh, boy. Wish I was a fly on that wall. Why, last time something like this happened was when your daddy and momma moved up the wedding date. They ended up eloping, you know."

Ryan's jaw slacked with surprise.

"You know what they say about people who live in glass houses," Gramps said. He chuckled under his breath.

Ryan shook his head. "But they act so…"

"Judgmental? Well, your daddy wasn't always like that, and I have to believe that deep down inside he's the same man he was when he left this farm. Your grandmother and I raised him up right with a foundation based on the good Lord."

"And Mother?"

"Aw, don't go believing those highfalutin ways of your mother's. I knew her when she was just a regular girl from Granby. She comes from a long line of simple folks." His grandfather gestured with his hands. "Why, her granny and mine were friends when their husbands were roughnecks on oil rigs."

Ryan grinned before his thoughts sobered again. "What should I do, Gramps?"

"Darned if I know. I'm old, but that doesn't mean I know everything."

"I always thought you did."

"Not me. I cheat. I turn to the good Lord when I don't know what to do. That's your answer, as well."

Ryan frowned.

"Pray, son. Pray like your life depends on it. Kait coming back into your life is nothing short of a marvel. A daughter, you say? Well, that's doubly marvelous. Don't let your folks stand in the way this time." Gramps pointed skyward with his thumb. "He has a plan. Up to you to figure out what it is."

Ryan took a deep breath. Gramps was right. It was time for some serious prayer. Time to ask for forgiveness for his mistakes and trust that the Good Lord would give him the wisdom and strength he needed for tomorrow.

Chapter Five

"When are we going to see Ryan again, Momma?"

"Tomorrow, I imagine. He said he was going to bring your kitten home."

Of course, that was before Ryan realized Jenna was his daughter.

Satisfied, Jenna's attention returned to her book. Kait was seated next to Jenna in the realtor's visitor area, waiting for the final printout of the house-sale contract. Jenna read while Kait reviewed the list the agent had compiled that afternoon.

Distracted, Kait flipped through the paperwork in her lap. She couldn't focus. Her mind kept wandering to Ryan. Surely he wouldn't disappoint Jenna because he was angry with Kait. Would he? The old Ryan wouldn't, but she wasn't sure she knew that Ryan anymore.

She closed the folder. The papers only depressed her. They were extensive lists of recommended updates and staging plans to prepare the house for sale. That translated to a lot of hard work and money on a house she wouldn't even be living in.

A lot of money she didn't have. Period.

The Granby real-estate market analysis had not been encouraging, either. The market was slow, so selling the house as is would not be an option if Kait wanted to get the most from the sale. Listing the house after repairs and staging still wouldn't provide any guarantees.

The agent had recommended leasing. That meant keeping her ties to Oklahoma.

No, it was better to proceed with the plans to prepare the house for sale as quickly as possible.

"Kait Field?"

A cold shiver skimmed over Kait. She looked up into the piercing, frosty-blue eyes of Elizabeth Delaney Jones. Ryan's mother.

"I don't know if you remember me," the older woman said.

Kait paused, so flustered she was unable to string together a quick response.

Was she serious? How Kait could forget her was the real question.

Once again, Kait was blindsided as an incident from the past raced through her mind.

Her hand moved to the chain around her neck, hidden beneath her blouse.

At her high-school graduation, Ryan's mother discreetly pulled Kait aside to congratulate her on achieving valedictorian—and in the same breath delivered a harsh warning not to get any ideas about her youngest son. While the Jones matriarch spoke, Kait had kept her left hand, bearing Ryan's promise ring, tucked inside the sleeve of her white commencement robe.

Kait straightened in her chair and pushed back her shoulders. Thank goodness she'd changed at the last minute into black slacks and a nice sweater for this appointment. Facing shantung silk and pearls while in her jeans and sneakers would have been even more difficult.

She took a deep breath and clutched her purse tightly. She was nearly twenty-eight years old now. A mother herself. Elizabeth Delaney Jones's threats couldn't touch her anymore.

Or could they?

"Of course I remember you."

"This is your daughter?"

"Yes."

Your granddaughter, Mrs. Jones.

But Kait would not introduce her to Jenna. Not now. Not like this.

"Jenna." Kait lowered her voice as she smoothed back her daughter's long hair. "Sweetie, can you go over there and see if you can find the crossword puzzle in that newspaper?"

"Okay, Momma."

Ryan's mother's eyes narrowed with speculation. Her mesmerized gaze followed the little girl as she walked across the room. Kait was never prouder of her beautiful daughter.

"I didn't expect to see you in Oklahoma ever again, Kait. I thought that was our agreement."

"We didn't have an agreement, Mrs. Jones. You spoke. I listened."

"You accepted my check."

Kait cleared her throat. "Mrs. Jones, my father recently passed away. I'm here to close out the family house."

"While I am sorry for your loss, forgive me if I am a bit skeptical about your intentions."

"Pardon me?"

"How long will you be in Oklahoma?"

"As I said, I'm here to sell my father's house."

"I see." She glanced to Jenna and then back to Kait. "It must be very difficult for you. A single mother. Perhaps I can help."

"Help?" Confused, Kait searched the other woman's face and blinked. Suddenly the meaning of her words was clear. Kait's head jerked back as though she'd been struck.

"I can offer a large enough incentive to keep

you and that little girl from wanting anything for a very long time."

Kait swallowed, her head spinning. Incentive? Incentive to go away? Incentive to pretend Jenna wasn't Ryan's daughter? There wasn't enough money in the world to cover all of that.

"Please," Kait finally breathed, biting back her anguish. "I'm not interested, nor do I need or want your money, Mrs. Jones."

The older woman lifted a shoulder in a gesture of dismissal and turned to go. Her parting barb, however, was right on target. "Very well. But my help certainly wasn't distasteful eight years ago, was it?"

Kait didn't bother to answer. There was no point trying to defend herself against someone who didn't want to hear the truth. The money that had been forced upon Kait eight years ago now sat in a savings account, untouched and collecting interest for Jenna's future.

Ryan glanced at his watch and cringed. Late.

His mother would wait for dinner, but she wouldn't be happy. Maybe tonight wasn't the time to tell them about Kait and Jenna.

He'd received the summons to appear at the Hill, his parents' Southern Hills home, early in the day, when he already had a full schedule of appointments booked well into the evening. It had taken some real finagling to move patients around in order to get here at all.

Ryan pulled his battered truck into the circular drive, behind his sister's gleaming black Lexus SUV and right behind a silver Mercedes-Benz sports coupe with temp tags. Luke's. Every fall Luke traded his "old" model in for an upgrade. Ryan inched as near as possible to the Mercedes-Benz, knowing his brother would truly be irritated when he saw the truck breathing the same air as his sportster.

He unfolded himself from the truck. Crossing his arms, he leaned against the hood of the vehicle and prepared himself mentally for an evening with his parents.

Before him stood the huge taupe stucco home, its sweeping stairs leading to a wide, pillared portico. Two massive terra-cotta pots overflowing with the last blooms of the season flanked the entrance. To the left, a towering magnolia guarded the property.

Ryan frowned. At times, he felt certain he'd been left on the Jones' doorstep by an errant kind person with a twisted sense of humor.

He supposed it could be attributed to spending so much of his childhood with his grandfather on the farm. Hanging out with Gramps had been his salvation.

The huge oak door at the top of the stairs

swung open, and his sister, Maddie, glared down at him, hands on her hips. "Have you decided yet?" she called.

"Decided what?"

"Whether you're coming in or not." She scrunched her nose and ran her fingers through her short blond curls in an impatient gesture that reminded him of her daughter, Faith.

"Funny."

"Get moving, would you? I'm starving."

"Yes, ma'am." He promptly took the steps two at a time to join his big sister at the door. Her gaze met his, and he recognized weariness and something else. Was it sympathy in those large green eyes? Ryan inhaled deeply as he realized.

She knew.

Whatever was going on inside, she knew. Maddie had no poker face. Her lips formed a tight line that said "don't ask, because I'm not telling."

"Faith here?" he queried, trying to get a handle on the drama about to begin.

"No. She's with the sitter."

Translation: this is family business. Maddie was a single mother, so if it was serious enough for her to spare precious time apart from her only child, tonight's dinner must be important.

He hesitated for a moment before following her into the house. If he was smart, he'd hightail it back to the clinic. Unfortunately that wasn't an option, so he'd go with the flow and see if he couldn't nudge this meeting along to a conclusion sooner rather than later.

"How's the job?" he asked.

"I'm miserable. Thanks for asking."

"You don't have to work for Dad and Luke, you know. There are other law firms in Tulsa."

"Right now they're the only law firm who will let me leave work in the middle of the day to go on field trips with my daughter's class."

"There is that."

"Besides, Dad's mellowed lately. He keeps encouraging me to do things with Faith that he never had time to do with his own kids."

"That's a good sign, right?"

"I suppose, but it's also a little unsettling."

"Yeah, I guess, but he's just hit the big five-o and now he's eligible for the senior discount at the diner. I suppose that makes a person stop and reevaluate their life."

Maddie stared at him for a moment, then laughed. "Very funny."

"Hey, I was being serious."

"Madeline, please bring your brother into the dining room immediately." His mother's perfectly modulated voice rang out like a sensing alarm the moment Ryan's booted foot stepped from the handcrafted Mexican tiles of the foyer to the pristine white carpet of the hall.

Most of the family had already seated themselves around the long, damask-covered table. His father, Lukas Jones Sr., seemed distracted as he pulled out his wife's chair at one end of the table and then moved to claim his own place at the head. Ryan's oldest sibling, Luke, sat across the table.

Ryan scooted his chair in closer to Maddie. Maybe this had something to do with his brother's bid for politics.

"New car, Luke?"

Luke nodded and picked up his linen napkin.

"Sweet. They cut you a deal because of that scratch on the rear bumper, huh?"

"What scratch?" Luke sputtered, eyes widening.

Ryan laughed at his brother's too-predictable reaction. When Luke's glance met his, Ryan winked. Maddie kicked Ryan's leg under the table.

"Ouch," he yelped.

"Grace, dear?" His mother interceded, nodding to her husband.

His father took Maddie's and his eldest son's hands and bowed his head. "Lord, bless this meal, and thank You for my family. We know

You will be with us as we face the decisions we are about to make. Amen."

Ryan squeezed his sister's hand at the end of the prayer, but she refused to acknowledge his silent question.

"Good of you to join us, Ryan," his mother commented as she waved Helen, their domestic of many years, in with the entrée.

Ryan eyed the steaming platter of baked pork chops that was placed on the table. "I had a choice?" He turned to Maddie. "You said be there or you'd break my kneecap."

"I did not. I merely said Mother and Father expected you."

"Same thing." He wasted no time helping himself to the large bowl of fluffy mashed potatoes. A home-cooked meal was a rare treat, and as long as he was here, he intended to fill his stomach.

Things remained quiet as the family passed serving dishes. Ryan glanced around, hoping someone would give him eye contact.

He nearly let his groan of frustration loose. They were apparently going to act the whole play out in choreographed and civilized order: dinner followed by dessert and coffee in the parlor. Then and only then would the "situation" be shared.

He couldn't do it. Not this time.

"Dinner looks delicious, Mother. Helen out-did herself. Now can you tell me what's going on?"

"I beg your pardon?" his mother replied. She smoothed her short silver-blond coif and examined her dinner plate.

There was way too much preoccupation with the Spode china tonight. A prickle of cold air raced up his spine.

Something was off.

And he couldn't figure out if it was him or someone else who was about to be put on the hot seat.

"We're going to have to talk now or I may get called back to work and miss out on whatever it is that has everyone looking like they need antacids."

His mother looked to his father to make the decision. Even Ryan was surprised at the success of his strategy. Prickles of unease raced down his arm, but he ignored the warning.

"Ryan," his father said. "Today your mother ran into Kait Field."

"Okay." He tensed and tamped down the screaming voice in his head. *Leave now, while you can.*

Reaching across the table, he nabbed the basket of golden croissants. "Please pass the butter."

"She has a child."

"Yes, Mother. I know. A sweet little girl named Jenna."

"Your mother believes Kait Field is going to claim that you are the father of her child." His father paused, cleared his throat and added, "We'd like to initiate paternity proceedings."

Ryan heard his father as he bit into the roll. He stopped moving like a movie in pause mode. When his brain kick-started again, he realized he'd forgotten to swallow. The fact was, he'd forgotten to breathe. Coughing, he reached for his Waterford and chugged down the icy water. "Excuse me?" He coughed again and stared first at his father and then his mother.

All around him his family kept talking, but their words sounded like they were far away and his thoughts continued to spin.

They knew? Was he the only one late to the party?

"Kait Field. That's the girl you went with in high school?" Maddie asked.

"They were merely acquaintances," Elizabeth Jones corrected her daughter. "It was fairly obvious she had a crush on Ryan. She followed him to OSU. With her background, I'm sure she saw your brother as, well, a way out of her situation."

Ryan's head reared back at the insult. "Whoa. Her background? Her situation? What are you talking about?"

"Her father was an unemployed alcoholic."

"He was a disabled vet, Mother."

She raised a brow.

"Mother, your memory has a few gaps. Kait was high-school valedictorian. She had a full-ride scholarship. Did you ever consider that maybe I followed her to OSU?"

"Ry, you aren't still interested in her, are you?" Luke asked. "I mean, she did dump you without looking back, right? Kind of shady that she should show up now, don't you think?"

Ryan leaned forward, his hands closing into fists. Half sitting, half standing, he stared his brother down. "What I think is that this isn't any of your business."

Luke's fork clattered to the table, and he held up his hands. "Whoa, Ryan. Calm down. I'm just saying."

Ryan eased back into the chair and glanced around. These people might be his family, but they never knew Kait. If anything, he should be the one under scrutiny, not Kait.

Never Kait.

"What exactly is going on here, Mother? What's the real reason you called this little meeting?"

"I'm concerned she may be back in town to take advantage of you. Your father and I would like you to find out what her agenda is. What she wants."

Ryan turned to his sister. "You agree with this?"

Maddie placed a hand on his arm and lowered her voice. "They're only trying to protect you, Ryan."

"Protect me? From what?" He looked at his mother. "Exactly what is it you think Kait wants?"

"Money, of course," his mother replied as she sipped her water. "It all boils down to money, dear. When she left town, I gave her a check to help her out. I think she's back for more."

Ryan inhaled sharply at the information. "A check? What check?"

"Maybe you should ask Kait."

"Are you telling me you knew, Mother? All this time—you knew?"

"As your sister said, we were only trying to protect you."

His father frowned absently. "DNA testing would resolve this."

"I don't need DNA testing."

"I think Ryan may be right."

To his surprise, the words were his mother's. "I'm right? That's a first. What are you saying, Mother?"

"I'm saying I am quite certain that before any

results are back that she will have agreed to a financial settlement."

"Seriously?" Ryan shook his head and pinned his mother with his gaze. "Look, to tell you the truth, I don't care what Kait's agenda is. Jenna *is* my daughter, and I don't need a paternity test to tell me that. Bottom line? I'm a lucky man to have gotten a second chance to be that little girl's father."

He glanced around the table yet again. "I want your support. Kait and Jenna are my family, too. Please don't make me choose."

"You're right, Ryan. I'm sorry," Maddie whispered.

"It's okay, Mads." He stood, placing his napkin on the table. "I have to go."

"Ry, wait." Luke stood also and reached his hand across the table. "You *are* right. All that really matters is that you're a father. Congratulations, little brother."

He accepted Luke's peace offering, then looked toward his mother and father. They didn't meet his gaze. Had they truly heard his plea? He hoped so, because telling everyone Kait and Jenna were his family had given him hope. More hope than he'd had in a long time.

Chapter Six

Ryan pulled the pickup into his driveway. The front light, normally on a timer, must have burned out, leaving shadows hovering around the walkway to the porch.

He got out of the truck and frowned. The little bungalow used to have a lot of curb appeal. Lately it simply looked abandoned. The yard needed serious attention, too. So why did he buy a home he didn't have time to maintain?

Simple. He needed a place for his animals: one dog, two cats, an assortment of lizards and turtles and yeah—possibly a partridge in a pear tree. If it wasn't for a Granby-city ordinance, he'd keep his horse here, too.

"Ryan."

He jumped at the voice that floated to him from behind the holly bushes, nearly causing him to drop the take-out dinner in his hand. *"Kait?"*

"I'm sorry. I didn't mean to scare you."

"I thought I was going to be mugged for my crab wontons," he mumbled.

Kait rose from the lawn chair on the front porch. He glanced away. He couldn't look at her without being bombarded with conflicting emotions.

"What are you doing out here?" he asked.

"I tried to call you several times, but you didn't pick up."

"I've been, ah, busy." Removing two flyers from the screen, he unlocked the front door. "Where's Jenna?"

"Molly Springer has her for the night. A sleepover with her grandkids."

He nodded and released a breath. Twenty-four hours later and he still ached like he'd fallen off his horse, been trampled and left bleeding in the dust. The disastrous dinner with his parents tonight had simply been another kick in the head when he was down.

He pushed the door open carefully, prepared to be assaulted. "Stay behind me. Jabez can be…exuberant."

"Who's Jabez?"

"Jabez is a cross between Big Foot and the Loch Ness Monster. He's a massive German shepherd–Heinz 57 mix."

The large dark dog began barking and whining as soon as the door was cracked open.

Kait made a noise of concern.

"Easy. Easy. Down, boy."

Jabez was a rescue hound and the best watchdog in the world—but only if the burglar was intent on stealing food. Anything else was pretty much fair game around the good-natured beast.

"No, boy. You don't like Chinese. Remember?" Ryan raised the white take-out bag in the air, then placed it on the foyer table before rubbing the drooling dog briskly behind the ears.

He turned, and Kait was still outside. "You can come in."

She chewed on her lip before opening the door and standing very still.

"What are you doing?"

"I thought you weren't supposed to make any sudden moves."

"That's a bear attack. I have food, so he isn't interested in you."

Kait nodded, looking unconvinced.

"What's this? Got a message for me?" Ryan removed the note attached to the back of the dog's collar, where even Jabez couldn't reach it.

"Your dog leaves you notes?" Kait asked.

"No. I have a high-school kid who comes by and feeds the animals in the evening and walks

Jabez. He used to leave notes on the table until we figured out that Jabez ate them."

"I see." Kait glanced around.

Ryan grimaced, his gaze following hers to the camera equipment, papers and mail scattered on the dining-room table and the clothes strewn over chairs, along with a pile of books stacked precariously on the floor. Good thing the light was out in the living room.

"My housekeeper is out of town this week."

"I'm not here to inspect."

Which left the obvious unasked question: Why was she here?

Ryan tossed a mangled throw toy into the darkness of the living room. Jabez raced after the flying object.

"Let's go in the kitchen."

Kait stopped to look at the framed photographs on the hallway wall before following Ryan. In the kitchen he scooped a pile of papers off the table and stacked them on the counter, next to a laundry basket.

"You want something to eat?"

"No, thank you," she said. "Do you mind if I sit down?"

"Course not. But be careful, there's usually a cat sleeping in one of those chairs."

Kait examined the chair before she slid into it.

Ryan reached for a soda from the refrigerator.

When he closed the door, a white card on the front of the refrigerator fluttered to the floor. Kait caught the paper and handed it to him, affording him a whiff of peach and apple blossoms.

She still wore the same perfume.

He paused, shaken, his mind a tumble of memories.

"Are you okay?" she asked.

"Probably not." He inspected the engraved wedding invitation before putting it back on the fridge with a magnet. Will Sullivan and Annie Harris. They were so in love. A sharp pain settled in the vicinity of Ryan's heart.

Well, one thing was certain—finding a date for a wedding now seemed the least of his concerns.

Why was she really here anyhow? What could she possibly say to make the situation better?

"How long were you outside?"

"Two hours."

He coughed. *"Two hours?"*

"You wouldn't answer the phone, and I didn't want to miss you. So I waited."

"What would you have done if I had spent the night at the clinic?"

Kait shrugged. "I didn't think that far ahead."

"What did you do for two hours?"

"I prayed." She cleared her throat and fiddled with her necklace. "A lot."

"Why were you praying?"

"I hoped you'd forgive me."

It took everything in Ryan to meet her eyes. They were clear, and it seemed as if he could see all the way to her heart.

Forgiveness? Didn't he need forgiveness, as well?

For moments they were both silent.

"Kait, I think we both want to move forward. The only way I know to do that is to lay it all on the table."

She nodded solemnly, her long lashes resting on her cheek as she stared at the floor. "You're right."

"Mind if I ask how my mother knows things I didn't know? Things I should have known?"

As though trying to find the words to explain, Kait swallowed and licked her lips. Her gaze met his. "I told my father I was pregnant, and he immediately called your parents. Your mother came to the house. She didn't believe me at first."

She twisted the silver chain in her hand.

"Didn't believe you?"

"Didn't believe you were the father."

Ryan closed his eyes at the humiliation Kait must have endured.

"At first, your mother wanted a paternity test. She said she'd sue me. But when my father made it clear he'd already disowned me, well, I guess she decided maybe the best thing was to help me get out of town. So she backed down."

"Oh, Kait," he groaned. "And where was my dad in all this?"

"I don't know. The only time I've ever seen your father was graduation."

Ryan folded his hands, striving to control his emotions. "What else did my mother say?"

"She said they had plans for you, and this would ruin your life."

He shook his head. "You being pregnant would ruin my life? What about your life, Kait?"

"My life was already a mess."

He clenched his jaw and shook his head. "So you're telling me that you sacrificed your future for mine?"

She pulled at a hangnail. "I suppose that's one way of looking at it."

"Is there another way?"

"Ryan." Her gaze met his. "I couldn't forgive myself if I was the one who stole your dreams from you."

He ran a hand through his hair. "What about you? What about your dreams?"

She began to respond and then closed her mouth.

"Kait, you were the valedictorian, with a full scholarship to O.S.U. You wanted to be a math teacher. And you gave it all up for our child. For me, too, I'm just realizing."

"I did what I had to do," she said. "I didn't have much self-confidence back then, and it's not like your parents ever approved of me to start with."

"Approved of you? What does that have to do with anything?"

"It may seem juvenile now, but our parents factored into things hugely back then. We both know we kept our relationship very much under the radar because we knew our parents had issues with us being together."

Ryan shook his head, irritated. "My parents knew we were seeing each other. They knew how I felt about you. Did you think I wouldn't have stood up for you?"

Kait was much too calm as her finger traced a circle on the surface of the table. She'd obviously thought about this many times over the years. "Look, I'm not accusing or blaming you or anyone else. I'm simply telling you how it was for me. I didn't exactly feel there was anyone supporting me except Molly."

"You didn't give me a chance to support you," he said softly, biting back bitterness.

"You're right." She met his gaze without backing down. "But I wasn't sure if, when push came to shove, your parents wouldn't win."

"Win?"

"Yes. Win. Your mother threatened to take the baby away from me if I stayed."

Stunned, he sucked in a breath.

"I left you a note because I couldn't tell you more," she said tightly, her voice finally revealing the pain of those memories. "I was afraid she'd find out. I was afraid she really would take our child."

"Oh, Kait."

"There's one more thing, Ryan."

He looked at her.

"Your mother handed me a check that day—a very large check. I didn't spend a penny."

"You should have."

"No. That was for Jenna. It's been collecting interest in the bank for eight years. I always thought it would be her college fund." Kait paused. "Ironic that her grandmother will be sending her to college, isn't it?"

Ryan stared blankly ahead. "You must think my family members are monsters."

"I didn't know what to think then, and I still don't now. Eight years ago I was confused and afraid. My father's drunken recriminations and your mother's threats only worsened the situation." Kait inhaled. "My world imploded that night."

The pain in her eyes was all too clear. He'd been acting like the injured party, but Kait had suffered far more injustice than he could imagine.

"Kait, I..."

She looked up.

"I want to apologize."

"You have nothing to apologize to me for."

"Yeah, I do. I was pretty harsh last night. You came to town to make things right, and I shot you down."

Kait didn't answer, but he could tell from the shadows beneath her eyes that she hadn't slept much more than he had last night.

"I wasn't in your shoes, and I shouldn't have made those judgmental comments." His thoughts went back to his conversation with Gramps. Judgmental. That's how he'd described his parents. Well, the apple hadn't fallen far from the tree, and he was by no means proud of himself. "I'm sorry, Kait."

"Consider it forgotten."

"I don't consider it forgotten. I know only too well how words can pierce. I'm truly sorry."

She nodded and glanced down.

"I won't lie to you. I wish a lot of things, mostly that you'd told me you were pregnant. But the way I choose to look at things now is that I have another chance to make things right." He paused. "Maybe if we work on it, little by little, we can get back to the place where we trust each other again. For our daughter."

Ryan placed his hand on hers, and Kait's lashes fluttered before her eyes met his. "And for us," he said.

Kait peered through the swishing windshield wipers at the familiar beat-up truck parked in front of the house.

"Who's that, Momma?"

"It's Ryan."

"Is he on the porch?"

She leaned forward and wiped the foggy window, trying to see through the moisture. "I think so. Got your umbrella?"

Jenna held up her pink umbrella and popped it open as she got out of the car.

Kait grabbed her grocery bags and dashed through the pelting rain to the front porch just behind Jenna. When her gaze met Ryan's guarded eyes, she glanced away, still feeling wary and vulnerable after last night's conversation.

Today he wasn't dressed as Dr. Jones, professional vet. No, he was all laid-back cowboy. A battered and faded denim jacket, collar turned up against the weather, completed his garb. He'd removed the straw Stetson, and his tousled hair looked as though he didn't own a comb. Yet he was all the more handsome and endearing for his usual charm.

Kait and Jenna shook the rain off their umbrellas and closed them.

"Ryan, this is a surprise," Kait said. The words sounded awkward and stilted to her ears.

He held up an animal carrier. "I got lucky. My last two appointments of the day canceled due to the flash-flood alert in Tulsa, so I brought by a friend of Jenna's."

"Kitty!" Jenna cried.

The kitten meowed. "She missed you, too," Ryan said. He smiled, and his gaze lingered on Jenna as though seeing her for the first time.

"Let's go inside," Kait said. She placed the groceries on the porch and inserted the key in the lock, pushing open the door.

Once they were inside the house, he handed the carrier over to Jenna and then got down on one knee so he was level with his daughter.

"Have you ever *had* a cat?"

"No."

He reached into his jacket pocket and pulled out a book. "*Basic Cat Care.*"

"Thank you." Jenna turned to Kait. "May I read it now, Momma?"

"Sure. Go ahead and take the kitten to your room."

"Want some help?" Ryan asked.

Jenna shot him an excited smile. "I'm okay."

He watched intently as she lifted the small carrier and headed upstairs.

"That's not exactly easy reading," he remarked to Kait.

"Jenna reads way above her grade level. I can barely keep her in books."

He frowned as though digesting the information. "I have a lot of catching up to do."

Kait didn't know what to say to that. Moments passed. Ryan shifted from one scuffed boot to the other.

"Would you like a glass of tea?"

"Sure, and how about I grab those groceries?" He opened the screen and scooped up the plastic sacks.

"Thank you."

Ryan followed her to the kitchen and glanced around. "The other night when I stopped by was the first time I've been in your house."

"Yes, I suppose that's true."

"Here okay?"

Kait nodded as he placed the bags on the counter.

"Don't you think it's odd that I had never been here?"

"Odd?" Kait slid a gallon of milk into the fridge. "Not any more odd than the fact that I've never been to your parents' home. We're two people from two different worlds."

The bottom line was his parents didn't like her, and her father didn't trust lawyers in general and the Jones family in particular.

Kait had always understood the ground rules.

"Why do you always point out our differences? I don't really think we're all that different." He frowned, his voice laced with irritation.

"Are you serious?" Kait opened a cupboard and stacked the cans inside.

"Yeah, I am."

"Ryan, when you and I left the door of school, that's where we left anything we had in common behind us."

"I disagree. Fact is, we both went home to empty houses. Neither of our parents were there for us, were they?"

She stared at him, surprised at the bluntness. "I guess that's one way of looking at it. But if it wasn't for my grandmother having paid for four years of private Christian schooling, I would have never ended up at the same high school as you to start with."

"Then I 'spose we should thank God for Grandma Redbird or we wouldn't have Jenna."

Kait couldn't help the small smile that escaped at his words.

Ryan leaned against the dishwasher. "What's this?" he asked, not shy about examining the list on the counter.

"Required repairs and changes the real-estate agent and I agreed upon before we list the house."

"I'll help."

"No." She shook her head. "I mean, no thank you." She was accustomed to tackling the problems in her life alone. Besides, working in close proximity with Ryan? Not such a good idea.

"So you have someone lined up?" The words were a slow drawl accompanied by an almost smug assessment, as though he already knew the answer.

"Not exactly. But I know how busy you are."

He raised a shoulder. "I'll find the time if it means I'll have an opportunity to be with my daughter more."

What could she say to that? He'd do it for Jenna. Isn't that what she wanted to hear? It wasn't his fault that she couldn't control the thumping of her heart when he was around.

Kait sighed.

"Come on. If it doesn't work out, you can have the satisfaction of firing me."

"I appreciate the offer. And the option clause. Thank you."

Ryan narrowed his eyes, an almost smile quirking up the corners of his lips.

She opened the refrigerator and eased a large pitcher of sweet tea to the table.

"Glasses?" he asked.

"Over the sink," Kait said. His casual familiarity was making her nervous. She was all too aware of Ryan's eyes still following each move she made. Getting the tea into the glasses with her hands shaking as they were was going to be surprising.

Kait slid a glass in front of him. "Thank you for everything you did for the kitten. Jenna is unbelievably thrilled to have her own pet."

"No problem. Every kid should have a pet. Of course, when I was growing up mine all lived at my grandfather's farm. So I know what it's like when your folks don't want an animal that might mess up the perfect order of things."

He took a swallow of tea and glanced at her. Kait crossed her arms.

"Kait. Please, sit down."

Ryan traced the moisture on his glass with a finger. He took a deep breath, and she saw fatigue settle over him.

Her heart contracted. The past twenty-four hours had been tough, especially for him.

"I want to ask you something."

She raised her brows.

"I'd like to take you and Jenna for a drive Sunday. I have to deliver a pup to my grandfather, and I thought it might be nice if we went."

"You don't have to include me, Ryan. I realize this is about you and Jenna."

"We were good friends once, weren't we?"

Kait lifted her face and gave him a small nod.

"You're the mother of my child. Can't we try to be friends again?" His gaze met hers. "Don't you think all three of us deserve that?"

She tucked her hair behind her ears. "Yes. Of course. I just meant— Well, you must have a lot of mixed feelings about me right now, and I want you to know that I completely understand."

"What I have is a lot more questions. But I'm a patient man, and I realized Monday night at about 3:00 a.m. how fortunate I am for this second chance. I'm not going to waste it on anger. I told you I want to move forward, and I mean that. Sitting in the past would make me crazy, and at this point, it's pretty much a short ride on an old pony."

She couldn't resist a small laugh at his words.

Ryan cocked his head and grinned. "You should do that more often."

"Laugh?"

"Yeah. It looks good on you."

Kait glanced away, flustered.

"So what do you think about Sunday?"

"I'd love to go with you and Jenna," she murmured.

"That's great." He nodded. "Really great."

Kait's gaze met his warm and welcoming green eyes. Yes. He was right. It was really great.

Ryan tapped on Jenna's door.

"Come in."

He stuck his head in the doorway. "Hey, Jenna."

"Oh, hi, Ryan."

She sat on her bed with the open cat-care book on her lap. The room was tidy, with the bed made and everything in its place. In the neatness department, she was so much like her mother that he wondered how he could possibly fit into their world.

"May I sit down?"

"Sure."

He pulled the chair from the desk and scooted it next to the bed.

"Did you know you have a great-grandfather who wants to meet you?"

Her eyes rounded as she picked at the threads of the quilt. She bit her lip in an expression that reminded him of Kait.

"A great-grandfather?"

"Yep. He's my grandfather and your great-grandfather. Pretty cool, huh?" he asked.

A shy grin began on Jenna face. It was as though she had simply been waiting for him to acknowledge her as his daughter.

As she looked up at him, her smile continued to stretch until it reached her eyes. She giggled with relief. "Uh-huh."

"I thought we'd all take a ride out to see him on Sunday."

"Momma said it was okay?"

"She did. So what do you think about all this, Jenna?"

"I'm happy."

"Me, too."

"I've wanted a daughter for a long time."

She cocked her head and stared at him. "You have?"

"I sure have."

"I've wanted a daddy for a long time, too, but I didn't want to make Momma sad."

"Do you think she's sad now?"

"No. She's not sad, but she does a lot of think ing."

"Huh." Ryan tucked the information away for later.

"Can I still call you Ryan for now?"

"Sure."

Jenna stretched her arm across the quilt and put her small hand in Ryan's before smiling sweetly up at him.

At that moment, the bitter regrets and anger he'd been holding on to faded away a little more. Maybe Gramps was right. He ought to save his anger for something worth being angry about.

He glanced at the picture on the wall. A family.

Right then he promised himself he would do everything he could to keep this little girl and her momma in his future.

Chapter Seven

"Tell me again where we're going?" Jenna said.

Ryan adjusted his ball cap and looked in the rearview mirror at Jenna, who was buckled safely into the backseat of the truck. "Why, we're headed to the country."

"Like another country?"

"Depends on who you ask." He laughed, the small dimple that appeared in his cheek only increasing his appeal.

Kait looked away. She couldn't help but notice how he was always laughing and exuberant around his daughter. And she couldn't deny that she longed to have that sort of easy relationship with him once again.

"I guess I better explain it better," he said. "You live in Philly. That's a city, like Tulsa. Granby is a town outside of the city. It's got a little bit of city and a little bit of country because there are places, like my friend Will's ranch, where you can ride horses."

Jenna appeared to be considering his words very thoughtfully.

"But where we're going, there's no city and the town isn't real close, either. It's miles and miles of land and trees with only a few houses here and there. In fact, where we're going used to be a working dairy farm."

"What's this country called?"

"Tishomingo."

"Tish-a-what?"

"Tishomingo."

Jenna repeated it back to him again.

"And your cousin Faith and her momma will be there, too."

When he turned to glance at her, Kait lowered her voice. "You should have told me your sister would be there."

"Would you have come?"

"Well, I...I don't know."

"Now you don't have to decide. Besides, we're almost there, and you wouldn't want to hurt an old man's feelings, would you?"

"You aren't that old."

Ryan's eyebrows shot up with surprise. "Oooh, good one, Kait. I think I see the old Kait Field coming back to us."

Kait kept her attention on her lap, trying hard

not to smile. She wasn't going to let him bull-doze her. He was wrong. The old Kait was gone forever, and the new Kait didn't back down.

"Whose truck is this?" she finally asked. The shiny black crew cab held every amenity of a luxury sedan.

"Oh, it's mine. There wasn't room in the Ford for Jenna. I only take this one out when I want to impress the ladies." He turned to Kait, his eyes crinkling at the corners. "Is it working?"

This time she couldn't hide a laugh. His light-hearted mood might be because of Jenna, but she was glad that all traces of the dark cloud she saw at his house had disappeared.

When he grinned back at her, she was grateful for Jenna's presence in the small space of the cab. Today Ryan appeared larger than life, and she couldn't avoid glancing at his hands on the steering wheel or the light dusting of hairs on his arms. Or staring at his profile as he drove.

The truck slowed, and they turned into a long gravel drive dotted with maple trees and lined with a cedar split-rail fence. "We're there."

"This is the farm?" Jenna asked, her nose pressed flat up against the glass as they continued up the road to the pale yellow, two-story house flagged by crape myrtle.

"Sure is. Not much going on here anymore,

but Gramps still keeps a cow or two and a pig and a few chickens. He also takes in my stray animals from the clinic when needed."

"Your grandfather lives here?" Jenna's eyes grew as wide as her grin.

Ryan nodded. Kait and Jenna both turned toward the big front porch.

"Look," Jenna cried out. "I see Faith."

"Yep. And that's her momma with her. Maddie. She's my sister." He stuck his head out the window and waved.

Kait stiffened, her hands tightening on her purse.

"What's wrong, Kait?"

"Nothing."

"Hey, I thought we were going to be honest from now on."

She bit her lip and gestured with her hands. "I'm nervous. Your family... I don't know if they..."

Ryan reached out and covered her hand with his. "Look at me."

Kait raised her head and slowly met his gaze, her heart beating rapidly in her chest.

"You're the mother of my child, and I won't ever let you down again."

Closing her eyes, she nodded, wanting desperately to believe him.

"You gonna take all day to come out of that

truck?" Grandpa Jones wasted no time. He moved down the steps to the gravel walk faster than a man in his eighties ought to be able to. Ryan's grandfather hadn't aged at all since the last time Kait had seen him. The moment she slid from the truck, he was there to greet her.

"We might." Ryan winked at Kait as hopped out of the truck and opened Jenna's door.

"Kait Field. Well, look at you. You're just as pretty as I remember." Grandpa Jones looked her up and down. "No. I believe you are prettier."

Kait smiled, only slightly nervous, and that was on principle. She hadn't seen Grandpa Jones in years, and however kind the man had been to her in the past, he was still a Jones. She wasn't certain how welcome she would be.

"Easy there, Gramps. You'll make her head so big, she'll have to ride home in the flatbed."

"Aw, don't listen to him. Is this Jenna?" He crouched down until he was eye level with the little girl and thrust out a hand. "How-do, young lady? I'm Grandpa Jones."

Jenna moved close to Kait's side as she extended her small hand to the old man.

"Why, you look just like your momma, don't you?"

Maddie slowly came down the stairs with Faith's hand in hers.

"Hello, Kait. I'm Ryan's sister, Maddie Callahan. I've heard a lot about you, but I'm not sure we've ever officially been introduced."

No, they hadn't met. Once again, the wide gulf between the two very different families was obvious. Madeline Jones had gone to an exclusive all-girl academy in Dallas during high school and to the East Coast for college, and while Kait had seen her at church, they certainly never ran in the same circles.

Today Maddie didn't look like another one of the Jones' family attorneys. She resembled Ryan, with an easy smile and unruly blond curls.

"I understand you've met this little tornado here," Grandpa Jones said with a nod toward Maddie's daughter.

Faith was as adorable as the first time Kait had met her. Today she was dressed in a yellow sweatshirt with a denim skirt, and her hair had been pulled into two small blond pigtails.

"Jenna is my friend," Faith told her mother.

Jenna grinned, delighted to be part of the group. Thrilled to belong to a family.

Ryan lifted the carrier from the flatbed. "Brought you that delivery, Gramps." A puppy stuck his little fawn-colored paw through the slats of the carrier and yapped.

"Puppy!" Faith cried.

"Ry, you know Faith can't have a dog," Maddie admonished. "We're not home during the day."

"Hey, this isn't your dog," Ryan said.

"That's right. This here is my pup." Grandpa Jones bent over to release the little pug from the carrier. "Aren't you a frisky feller?" The puppy proceeded to chase its short corkscrew tail. "What do you say, girls? What should I name him?"

"Why is his face all flat?"

"That's just the way God made him, Faith-girl."

Jenna giggled when the puppy snorted. "He sure breathes funny."

"He does sound funny, doesn't he?" Grandpa Jones said. "What do you say we name him Buster?"

Both girls laughed.

Ryan put a leash on Buster and handed the dog to Jenna. "See that gate over there?"

Jenna nodded.

"Gramps has a little penned-in yard back there. You take Faith and Buster and play for a bit. Take the leash off while you play. And don't let either one of them out of the gate until you're done playing. Okay?"

"All by myself?" Jenna's eyes rounded.

"Why sure, you're a big girl. You did say you're almost eight, right?"

Her head bobbed in reply.

"Besides, we'll be right over there on the porch."

Ryan knew just the words to say to make a little girl smile.

"I can do that?" Jenna glanced to Kait for approval as the energetic puppy raced back and forth.

"Why, of course you can," Ryan repeated. He turned to Kait. "She'll be fine."

"Go ahead, Jen. Ryan's right. You're a big girl."

Jenna released a breath and laughed.

"So Buster is another one of your strays?" Maddie asked.

"Yeah. A woman came in with Buster last week. She apparently discovered her kids are allergic to cleaning up after him."

"That's so irresponsible," his sister replied.

"Happens all the time. He's a cute pup, and I knew Gramps here was looking for a new addition to the family since his dog passed on."

Gramps called to them from the porch. "I've got fresh strawberry lemonade here." He gestured to a table nestled in the corner of the shady porch and a large crystal pitcher filled to the rim with lemonade and sliced strawberries. Next to the pitcher was a tray of glasses.

Ryan led the way to the porch, and Kait followed.

"Drink?" he offered.

"Yes. Thank you."

Kait sat on the settee, leaving plenty of room for Ryan, hoping he'd read the pleading message in her eyes as he handed her a filled glass. She silently begged him not to leave her alone.

He grinned and obliged, his long legs stretched out in front of him as he settled back on the cushions, an arm along the back nearly touching her shoulder. She shivered with the awareness of his proximity.

Kait gazed out at the farmland before her, willing herself to relax. Several old barns dotted the horizon, along with an orchard in the distance. Overhead the sky was clear and cloudless blue, and the only sound was the laughter of their children.

"That's a lovely girl you have there, Kait," Grandpa Jones said as he gently set his rocking chair into motion.

"Thank you," she returned. "The lemonade is delicious."

"Thank you, back at you." The older man grinned, a mischievous twinkle in his eyes, not unlike his grandson's. They both had the same crinkle lines, except Grandpa Jones's were etched deeply into his tanned face.

"All this politeness is making me nervous. How 'bout you?" he asked.

Taking a sip of lemonade seemed the only thing to do, since she didn't have an answer to his question.

"You got to be a mite uncomfortable sitting here like you're being interrogated," the older man continued.

She choked on her swallow, and Ryan quickly raised a hand to pat her back.

"A little," she finally admitted, easing the tension.

"Well, don't be. We're all family."

Kait released a breath, conscious of Ryan's warm palm still resting on the small of her back.

"You know, the more I look at Jenna, the more I see how much she actually looks like her daddy."

Ryan's head whipped up. "Gramps."

"What?" He looked from Ryan to Kait. "All I'm saying is the Joneses and Fields make some right handsome children. A man can never have too many great-grandchildren. Right, Maddie?"

"Leave me out of this one, Gramps. More lemonade, Kait?"

"I'm fine, thanks." Kait's gaze followed Faith and Jenna playing on the grass. "Your daughter is adorable. How old is she?"

"Five going on sixteen. She's just like her father. Completely fearless."

"We lost Faith's daddy before she was born," Grandpa Jones added.

"I'm so sorry," Kait said.

Maddie jumped up, her attention on her daughter as the little girl tussled with the small dog, pulling his tail. "Young lady, stop teasing that dog."

"Yes, Momma." Faith hid her little hands behind her back and rocked from side to side, smiling.

"That child."

"Why, Faith's the spitting image of you when you were a little girl. Acts just like you, too."

Maddie frowned. "Inherited orneriness doesn't make it right, Gramps."

Grandpa Jones released a hearty laugh.

Maddie sat down and looked at Kait. "I'd love it if Faith and Jenna could get together for a play date before you leave."

"Really?" Kait's surprised glance met Maddie's green eyes.

"Of course. They are cousins, after all."

After all. Gratefulness filled Kait's heart.

"Thank you, Maddie. I'd like that."

"How long are you and Jenna fixin' to stay in Oklahoma?" Gramps asked.

"I'm not exactly sure," Kait answered. She

wasn't really evading the question; she truly wasn't sure. "I have to empty out my father's house first."

"I'm sorry for your loss," Grandpa Jones said with a shake of his head.

"What is it you do in Philly?" Maddie asked.

"I'm the office manager of a small medical practice."

"No kiddin'," Gramps said. His eyes lit up. "You hear that, Ryan?"

"Yeah, Gramps. I heard her."

"Momma?"

Kait turned. "Yes, Jen?"

"There's a cow over there. A real, live cow. May I go see her?"

Kait looked to Ryan.

He grinned. "Sure, come on. We'll take them both to see Gramps's last Holstein." He took the glass from Kait, then held out his hand to help her up from the low-sitting swing.

"Thank you," Kait said. She glanced away, certain everyone could see her heart doing little pirouettes at the contact of Ryan's hand on hers.

"Take them for a walk down the road to see that old goat next door," Gramps called.

"Your neighbor has a goat?" Kait asked.

"Naw, it's my neighbor I'm talking about.

Owns the apple orchard down at the end of the field."

Kait swallowed a laugh and glanced around, but apparently she was the only one who found Gramps's comment out of the ordinary.

"Maddie, you should go along with them. Mayhap that grandson of hers that's sweet on you is visiting."

"Gramps," Maddie warned.

"Jenna, you and Faith take that basket from the picnic table," Gramps called. "Pick some apples while you're out there."

"Won't his neighbor mind if we pick her apples?" Kait asked once they were out of earshot.

"Naw, Gramps has been courting Mrs. Wyatt for years."

"Really?"

"Yep. One of these days she's going to say yes." Ryan took her hand in his, lacing their fingers. "Better hold on to you, the ground is a little uneven from here to the orchard and you're wearing those fancy shoes."

Kait glanced down at her flats, perplexed. "These aren't fancy shoes."

"No?" He shrugged. "Then I guess I was looking for an excuse to hold your hand."

Kait opened her mouth then closed it, confused and pleased at the same time.

* * *

"Grandpa Jones said I could call him Gramps," Jenna announced from the backseat of the truck.

The sun had almost set as they headed down the highway toward Granby.

"Yes, he did," Ryan said.

"And he showed me all the pictures in his big photo album."

"Did he?" Ryan glanced in the mirror and smiled.

"I've never had a Gramps before." Jenna yawned. "Can we go back again? He said he'd teach me how to fish."

"Whoa. No kidding? You know, Gramps doesn't offer to teach just anyone how to fish. You must be special."

"Really?"

"Yep." He grinned. "Last person he taught to fish was me."

"Momma, do you know how to fish?"

"I used to. Ryan taught me a long time ago."

He glanced over at Kait. She remembered. Some of the best days of his life were sitting with Kait talking and fishing. He'd steal a few kisses whenever he thought he could get away with it. And he thought he could get away with it more often than not.

Ryan grinned and couldn't help glancing over

at Kait's mouth. Those were kisses worth remembering, too.

But did *she* remember them?

Their eyes met in the semidarkness of the cab, and he was certain she blushed before she glanced away.

"What do I need to go fishing?" Jenna asked. Her voice was subdued as she fought sleep.

"We'll get you a permit and a pole. Of course, you have to have a fishing hat," Ryan said.

"A hat?"

"The best fishermen have fishing hats. That's the secret to good fishing."

Jenna giggled.

They drove the rest of the way in silence, Ryan occasionally glancing at Kait, wondering what was going on in her head. He knew by the set of her chin she was thinking hard about something. Kait was always thinking.

When he pulled the truck to a noiseless stop at the curb in front of the Field house, he glanced into the backseat. "She's out."

His eyes met Kait's.

"A long day," he added.

Kait smiled at the sleeping child, her heart overflowing with love. "Probably the best day of her life, too."

"You think so?"

"I know so."

He cleared his throat, knowing what he was about to say might upset her, but it had to be said so he was willing to take the risk. "No pressure, Kait, but you know, you could always stay in Oklahoma. I can promise many more days like this."

"Please don't make it any harder for me than it already is, Ryan."

"It doesn't have to be hard. Jenna would love living here. Why, I've got a horse at Will Sullivan's ranch that she could ride. Bet she'd love that."

"That's not fair. I can't compete with what you can offer Jenna."

Ryan stared ahead, pierced by her words. "This isn't a competition," he murmured.

"I'm sorry. I shouldn't have said that."

He gave a slow nod, trying to move past the sting of her words. "I know we haven't talked about custody yet, but I was pretty clear that I want to spend more time with Jenna. Have you thought about her staying here in Granby?"

"Staying here?" Kait tensed, and her face paled.

"Easy, Kait, I don't mean I'm trying to take her from you or anything."

"Well, I guess she could come here for some of her school vacations. The two of you together, that's a good thing."

"The three of us together wouldn't be so bad either, would it?"

Kait frowned. "We were talking about you and Jenna."

He released a breath of frustration and glanced up at the dark sky through the window before turning toward Kait. "Look, I'm not trying to make things difficult. Wait until you have time to sort it all out. All I want you to do is think about what I'm saying."

"I guess I'm confused. Think about what exactly?"

"Kait, I'm asking you not to rule out living in Granby."

Though she nodded, Ryan sensed her sadness. Why did it have to be like this? Either-or. Why couldn't they all be together? He swallowed the bitterness that threatened to rear its head. No. He wouldn't go there again.

"Thanks for coming today, Kait. I know I sort of lassoed you into a Jones family day, but it meant a lot to my grandfather."

"It meant a lot to Jenna and me, as well."

"Yeah?"

"Of course. Family is very important. And mine hasn't always been so disconnected. When my father died, I realized how very much Jenna needs her father. I should have realized that sooner." Kait licked her lips. "I also realized that if anything happened to me, Jenna would be alone in the world."

Ryan stilled at her words.

"This time in Oklahoma means everything to Jenna. She's finding out who she is. Not a day goes by that she doesn't start counting on her fingers how many new relatives she has."

He sighed. "Most people take family for granted."

Kait nodded. "How did Maddie lose her husband?"

"He was a police officer. It was in the line of duty."

She winced.

"Yeah. It was a difficult time all the way around."

"What was all that teasing your grandfather was doing about his neighbor's grandson?"

"We played with the Wyatt kids every summer when we were growing up. Susan, the oldest, is now an orthopedic surgeon at St. Francis. Ben is the youngest. Ben always had a crush on Maddie the size of Texas, though he hardly ever said two words to her. Not sure how Maddie felt about him."

He slid out his side of the truck and carefully opened the back door of the cab. "I'll carry her in."

They crossed the lawn to the front stoop, and

Ryan stood with one foot on the step and one on the sidewalk while Kait dug for her keys. He glanced down at the bundle in his arms. The little girl's face was serene in the light of the porch lamp. Gramps was right; she was the best of them—a perfect combination of a Jones and a Field. He could see Kait in the bow of her lips, the long eyelashes and the high Cherokee cheekbones. She had his nose, his freckles and, sadly, his ears.

Their daughter.

Ryan swallowed and looked away for a moment. His heart ached, yearning for what could be.

Lord, please help Kait see this is where she belongs.

Chapter Eight

~

Kait pushed open the door to the attic. "Be careful, Jen. That doorway is low. Watch your head."

"I will." Jenna's eyes rounded as she climbed the stairs in front of Kait. When they reached the top, she grabbed for her mother's hand. "It's kind of scary up here, isn't it?"

"Attics are just big closets. Let me find the light."

She grabbed the string hanging from the ceiling and pulled, jerking on the single bulb, which set it swaying. The light came on all right: however, it didn't illuminate nearly as much as Kait recalled. The shadows loomed larger as the bulb continued to move back and forth.

Overhead, a heavy thump shook the attic walls.

Jenna gave a small scream and wrapped her arms around Kait's waist. "What was that?"

"Oh, honey, it's okay. That's Ryan. He's on the roof patching the leaks." Kait moved to the small circular attic window. She rubbed the glass with her flannel shirttail, wiping away cobwebs and years of grime. "See his truck down there?"

"But if he's on the roof, he might fall off."

Kait swallowed. She, too, had been more than a little anxious about Ryan on the roof of the foursquare with its double-dormer roofs. But he'd only groaned when she voiced her concerns.

"Ryan says he knows what he's doing."

"Does he?"

"I hope so."

Jenna looked around the space of the attic and frowned. "I think I want to go downstairs and play with Kitty and read."

Kait chuckled. "Okay. I don't blame you. Leave the door to the attic open, and call if you need me. Remember, Faith's mother is coming to pick you up after lunch."

"Aunt Maddie." Jenna grinned.

"Yes. Aunt Maddie."

"I remember. I'm so excited."

"Me, too, sweetie."

As Jenna's footsteps faded away down the steps, Kait walked around the small attic, assessing the boxes and old furniture.

A chest of drawers to her right caught her attention. Though scarred in places, the bureau was obviously a quality piece of furniture. Kait blew a layer of dust off the top, then ran a hand over the smooth dark wood, her fingers tracing the delicate scroll work. Grabbing the porcelain knobs, she tugged on the top drawer. Years of Oklahoma humidity kept the wood stuck in place. The wood yielded only an inch at a time as Kait wiggled it back and forth.

Once the drawer was halfway open, the sharp aroma of mothballs wafted into the room, causing her nose to twitch as she assessed the neat rows of crisp white pillowcases all adorned with baby blue hand-crocheted trim. The delicate handiwork belonged to her grandmother. She had forgotten these treasures were here.

The second and third drawers held tea-dyed doilies and crocheted dresser scarves. Again, they were all made by Grandmother Redbird. What an incredible skill. Kait's thoughts returned to her childhood and the hours spent at her grandmother's knee, listening to stories and watching the clicking needles in her grandmother's lap.

They weren't simply drawers full of heirloom linens. They were drawers filled with their heritage. A little bit of Kait and Jenna's past seemed to unfold each day, bringing them closer to each other and their heritage.

She couldn't wait to show the linens to her daughter.

Kait glanced around. A tall cherry armoire stood in the corner of the space. She didn't hesitate to unlatch the brass lock of the door, causing the clothes inside to burst from their confines. Her mother's wedding dress was front and center, zipped into a stiff plastic storage bag. The white satin had faded to a soft cream, which only enhanced the elegant gown. Kait carefully unzipped the bag. Tiny satin buttons ran down the back. The bodice and long-sleeve cuffs were adorned with intricate hand-sewn beadwork.

Kait was about Jenna's age when her mother first told the story of how she met her father when he was on leave from the army. They were married before he returned to his duty station overseas. Four weeks. A whirlwind courtship.

Love at first sight. Not many people believed in that, but Kait did.

She touched the chain at her neck, pulling it from where it lay hidden beneath her long-sleeve T-shirt. She examined the rings dangling on the end—her mother's wedding band, engagement ring and Kait's own promise ring from Ryan.

So much love surrounded the three rings. So much hope. Kait continued to wear them close to her heart because deep down inside, she still believed in love.

Slowly closing the bag, Kait pushed the plastic back into the closet and locked the door. When she turned around, all the carefully labeled stacks of boxes pushed against the wall began to speak to her with a loud cacophony.

Open me. Come here, I have a story to tell you. Remember?

Suddenly the magnitude of what she was doing hit. Overwhelmed, Kait sat down on the dusty floor and closed her eyes. Returning to Oklahoma wasn't just about Jenna. The trip was also about making peace with her past.

Making peace? What had she been thinking? Everything had seemed so simple when she'd planned it in her head weeks ago in Philly.

Now it was anything but.

Why did she feel like she was trying to cut ties to her past? She raised her head and once again glanced at the boxes.

Coming home had only made her more confused than ever.

As it was, she still couldn't bring herself to go into her father's room, choosing instead to sleep in the guest bedroom. She still lacked the courage to face Jack Field.

Disappointing her father hurt as much as what she'd been forced to do to Ryan, to their love.

"Lord, I know You've forgiven me. But now I ask for the courage and the strength to do what I need to do. Whatever that may be. Help me face the future You have for me."

Kait took a deep breath and turned to the boxes. She began to sort them into three piles. Boxes that were definitely going to the trash, items for charity and boxes she didn't have the emotional fortitude to go through right now.

Moving to her knees, she pulled a familiar carton across the dusty wood-plank floor toward the middle of the room. Tentative at first, she slipped her fingers under the flaps, unfolding the top enough to peek inside and glimpse the blue-and-yellow fabric.

Her mother's quilt.

She'd completely forgotten this box was up here. Kait quickly delved into the box, removed the quilt from the plastic and burrowed her nose in the soft folds.

Lavender.

Each corner of the quilt had a pocket for a small lavender sachet. Kait pulled one out and rubbed the satin pouch back and forth between her fingers, crumbling the dried flower. Released, the scent drifted into the air and surrounded her.

"Oh, Mom." Kait hugged the quilt to her and slowly rocked back and forth. "How I miss you."

"Everything okay up here?"

Ryan.

"Yes." She swiped at the moisture on her face with the back of her hands and tucked the necklace into her shirt.

His heavy steps moved up the stairs. "The roof wasn't as bad as I thought. Only one significant area, and it's patched already. We'll know for sure when the next big rain hits. I guess I'll repair the ceiling and repaint after that."

He ducked the low-hanging beams as he crossed the attic. The closer he got, the more the breadth of his shoulders seemed to fill the room. Kait concentrated on folding the quilt. She cleared her throat. "Thank you so much."

"No problem." He walked to the window, hands in his jeans pockets, and stood looking out. "Quite a view up here."

"I know. When it's clear, you can see the Tulsa skyline if you look really hard."

"So where'd that ugly sign on your front lawn come from?"

Kait got up and walked to the window. "Oh,

that." She glanced at the For Sale sign. "The Realtor dropped it off while you were on the back part of the roof."

"But the house isn't ready. You've got more problems in this place than solutions."

She sighed. "Don't remind me."

"Well, someone has to." He released a breath. "Getting this house market ready in less than three weeks just plain isn't going to happen, Kait."

"I know that, but the Realtor is hoping to get someone interested in a fixer-upper."

Ryan snorted, his opinion on the subject clear. He turned on his booted heel and inspected the attic. "Those boxes need to go someplace?" He nodded toward the pile shoved near the stairs.

"They go to charity."

"Front hall okay with you for now?"

"Yes. Thank you."

He began the trek down the stairs, mumbling as he went.

"Did you say something?" she asked.

"No, I'm just talking to myself."

"What about?"

"You don't want to know," he muttered. "Trust me."

Fifteen minutes later, he stood in front of her as she sat on the floor going through another box.

"Anything else?"

"Not yet."

He glanced at the armoire that held her mother's wedding dress. "Beautiful piece of furniture. You aren't going to get rid of it, are you?"

She sighed. "I don't know what I'm going to do yet."

"Mind if I look inside?"

"No, of course not. Go ahead."

Turning the brass key, he opened the door and smiled at the wedding dress that jumped out to greet him. "Your momma's?"

"Yes."

"I recently found out my parents eloped." He shook his head and gave a half smile of wistful amusement.

"Oh?" There was obviously more to the story, but she wasn't going to ask.

When he moved the wedding dress aside, a flash of deep burgundy appeared in the closet. "Hey, is that your prom dress?"

Kait got up from the floor and crossed the room to the armoire. She reached behind the plastic bag protecting the wedding dress. "I guess it is. Funny, I didn't see it earlier."

"How could you miss it?"

She smiled. He was right. At seventeen it was more dress than she'd ever seen and definitely more than she'd ever worn.

The dress was a teenager's dream, with its satin spaghetti straps, frothy chiffon overskirt and tulle crinoline. Somewhere in the attic boxes were her pressed corsage and a photo of her and Ryan in their finery.

"Remember prom?" he asked.

How could she not? They had been so much in love. Ryan gave her the promise ring that night. Kait's head had been far, far away in the clouds. Emotion filled her as the memories tumbled back.

"We can't go there, Ryan," Kait whispered, her voice raw.

Ryan turned to her. "I'm not asking you to go back. I just don't want to ever forget, either."

Forget? She had a child now. No, she wouldn't likely forget. With her gaze fixed on the armoire, her fingers fumbled as she tried to lock the door.

Ryan moved closer. "Let me help."

"I don't need any help."

He slipped the key from her fingers anyhow and locked the door. Kait turned away, trying to compose herself.

When **his hand** touched her hair and gently stroked **the locks** before resting a comforting hand on her back, she relaxed a fraction, longing to lean into the strength of him but not daring to.

"I'm sorry," he murmured. "I didn't mean to upset you."

"I'll be fine."

"Yeah, you will. You're always fine, aren't you?"

She gave a halfhearted nod.

"Kait, pride isn't a badge of honor." He shook his head. "Why can't you let me in? Just a little."

She turned to face him, surprised at his sudden outburst.

"I don't want to…" Frustrated, she sighed and tried again. "I don't want to obligate you. I've barged into your life and turned it upside down. The last thing I want is for you to feel obligated. To Jenna, yes. She's your daughter—but not to me."

"I can tell you right now that what I feel for you is not obligation. That word has never crossed my mind."

Kait frowned at his words, knowing that Ryan was too much the white knight, always doing the right thing. He might not feel obligated, but he'd never knowingly do anything that wasn't honorable. She'd never know if he was acting out of regard for her or simply doing the right thing for his daughter's mother.

She dared to turn her head and meet his gaze.

"We're starting to get a handle on both of us being Jenna's parents, but what about us, Kait?"

"Are you asking where we go from here?"

"I guess I am," he said. "Maybe you should start giving it some thought."

"The pizza man is here!" Jenna called.

"Tell him we're coming," Ryan answered. His questioning eyes never left hers as he stood waiting for a response.

Kait nodded. Ryan was right. It was time for her to think about exactly what she wanted from her daughter's father.

Ryan set his watch and cell on the counter as he turned on the faucet and washed his hands. "I put a surprise in the freezer."

Jenna opened the freezer door. "Ice cream?" Her eyes widened with delight, and she looked back at him.

"Not just any ice cream. Tell her, Kait."

Kait peeked over Jenna's head. "Oh, my. Look at that." She assessed the familiar purple-and-blue containers in the freezer. "He's right, Jen. Braum's ice cream is wonderful."

She turned to Ryan. "That's a lot of ice cream."

"Naw, just a mint chocolate chip for Jenna, and…" He paused and looked her up and down. "You still look like butter pecan to me."

Jenna laughed at his antics.

Butter pecan. Yes. That was still her favorite. Kait pulled the dishes from the cupboard and turned, nearly running into Ryan, who was right behind her, ready to take them from her hands and place them on the table.

"Got it," Ryan said, his fingers grazing hers. He grinned as though he knew the havoc his touch created.

Did he? Or was that grin just Ryan being Ryan?

Unsettled, Kait slid into a chair next to Jenna. "Do you want to pray?"

Jenna nodded, and they held hands around the table.

"Dear Lord, thank You for this food and for all my new family. Amen."

Kait opened her eyes and met Ryan's gaze. Her breath caught as he squeezed her fingers before he slowly opened his hand and released her.

When the pizza box was opened, the spicy scent wafted through the air. Kait inhaled deeply. Each slice was slathered with rich tomato sauce and mozzarella, then crowned with large disks of pepperoni and round marbles of sausage. "Oh, my goodness. Mazzio's Pizza."

"The best in the whole wide world," he said.

Jenna laughed. "The whole world?"

"Yep. Tell me they have pizza this good

in Philly," Ryan said once they'd finished several bites.

"Okay, maybe not," she conceded. "But they do have great brick-oven pizza back home."

"Back home? What are you talking about? This is your home." He waved a hand over the table. "And this is what you've been missing."

"Momma, I really think this *is* the best pizza I have ever had."

"Atta girl," Ryan said, reaching over to ruffle the young girl's bangs.

Jenna gave him an adoring smile in return.

Kait noted the exchange. The dynamics had completely changed. Now it was two to one, and she was the odd one out. Jenna had found herself a hero in Ryan.

She sighed. Leaving Oklahoma would be difficult—for all of them.

"You okay?" Ryan asked.

"Me? Oh, yes. I was thinking."

"About pizza, right?" He winked at Jenna before he stood and straddled the chair as he reached into the box. "More?" He nodded toward their plates.

"We haven't even finished our first piece," Kait said.

"Slowpokes. My turtles eat faster than you."

"You have turtles?" Jenna asked. "I thought you just had a lizard."

"Are you kidding? I have more animals at my house than at the zoo."

"Now you're the one kidding," Kait said.

"Just a little." He turned to Jenna "But I do have turtles. Fred and Ethel are red-eared sliders. They have their own tank, right next to Roscoe the lizard."

"Fred and Ethel?"

"Yep. And I have cats and a beast dog, too."

"Can I see them?"

"I bet we can arrange that, right, Kait?" Ryan answered.

Kait shook her head. Someone was going to have to talk to him about riding roughshod over the rules. Didn't he know you don't make promises to children that you might not be able to keep?

"Can we, Momma?"

"May we. And yes, we'll see if we can arrange that before we leave Oklahoma."

Jenna nodded, slid her chair back and rubbed her tummy. "I'm so full. May I be excused?"

"Sure, sweetie. Wash your hands."

"Okay." Jenna smiled. "Thank you for the pizza, Ryan."

"You are very welcome."

Jenna looked intently at Ryan. "I really can see your animals, right?"

"I never break a promise."

Kait waited until Jenna was out of earshot before addressing Ryan. "You have to be careful about promises. Kids take them very seriously."

Ryan set his drink down. "Kait, I take promises very seriously, too." He stared into her eyes. "I keep mine."

Kait glanced away. The reference was very clear.

He stood, walked to the refrigerator and examined the calendar. "Let's plan right now. Dinner at my house. You, me, Jenna, Jabez, Chester, Fred and Ethel and the rest of the gang."

"Ryan, I'm sorry. I didn't mean to sound—well, you know."

Ryan turned to her. "You don't need to apologize. I get that your job as Jenna's mother is to protect her. You do that well." He frowned. "Maybe too well."

"Thanks for understanding."

"I do. But I'm serious. You and Jenna for dinner."

"I didn't know you could cook."

A slow grin lit up his face. "I can't. But I don't let little things like that stop me anymore."

She couldn't help but laugh.

"We've both changed, haven't we?" he remarked.

"Yes. I guess we have. But change is a good thing. It takes courage."

"You're right. Though I'd say you have far more courage than I do, Kait."

She blushed beneath his scrutiny.

"By the way, Gramps called today."

Kait raised a brow.

"He invited us to the farm a week from Sunday for a birthday party. He'll be eighty-four. I didn't say yes or mention it to Jenna without talking to you first."

"You want to take Jenna?"

"He specifically invited you, too."

"Who else will be there?"

"Kait, it's his birthday. My entire family will be there."

"Oh, Ryan." Her stomach churned.

"My parents need to meet Jenna."

"Your mother doesn't like me."

"My mother doesn't like anyone."

"Now you're exaggerating."

"Not really."

Kait pursed her lips. She didn't want to argue with him, but there didn't seem to be a compromise.

"Can't you do this for Jenna? She needs to meet her grandparents."

"I agree, but I still don't think I can. Even for Jenna. You'll have to take her yourself."

"I don't get it. What's between you and my mom?"

"Your mother has always made it painfully clear I wasn't good enough for you."

"She's wrong. You're way too good for me. Always have been. But what does that matter now?"

"Oh, it matters."

He glanced at the wall clock. "I've got to go. Can we talk about this again?"

"Sure. But don't get your hopes up that you'll change my mind."

"What was all that talk about change and having courage?"

"Not fair," she said.

They were silent as she walked to the front door with him. Ryan's expression became serious as his gaze met hers. "Kait."

"Hmm?"

He pushed open the screen door. "All I'm asking is for you to pray about going."

She frowned. "I'll think about praying about it."

"Kait."

"I'm being honest. Right now that's the best I can do."

Ryan nodded. "Fair enough, then."

"Thank you for all you did around here today."

"You're welcome. The gutters are next."

"Does cleaning the gutters involve being on the roof again?"

"Well, yeah. That's the only way to get the job done."

"I'm not crazy about you being up there," she said.

"Worried about me?" He raised his brows.

"I'd be concerned about anyone on my roof."

He shook his head, shooting her an expression of disappointment.

"Don't think I don't appreciate your help, Ryan. I really do. Thanks to you, we're whittling that list down quickly."

"Kait, I'm not here because I'm looking for your appreciation."

She searched his eyes, trying to understand what he was saying. Then she realized it was his daughter he was talking about. "Jenna. Yes. I understand."

"No. I don't think you do. I'm here because I believe in something much bigger than just that little girl. I believe you and I have a dance to finish."

Kait put her hand to her heart as she turned away from the door. A dance to finish? She bit her lip. Did she dare hope he meant that they might be more than just Jenna's parents?

"Anyone home?"

Kait recognized that voice. She dried her hands and rushed to the foyer.

Molly Springer smiled from the other side of the screen. A department-store shopping bag dangled from one hand and a leather bag was slug on her shoulder. Molly looked as elegant as ever and nothing like a grandmother of ten. Tonight her gray hair was pulled back with silver combs. Silver and turquoise earrings dangled at her ears, accenting her exotic Native American features. She filled out her black jeans and Southwestern print silk blouse like a woman half her age.

Kait opened the screen door. "Molly, what a nice surprise."

She dropped the bag and her purse and collected Kait into a warm embrace. "I just stopped by to check on you."

"Do I need checking on?"

"Oh, you know what I mean. We never have a minute to chat when the kids are around. As it is, I only have a minute now."

"Come in and have a seat, at least."

"I hope I'm not interrupting. I was going to call." Molly waved a hand, and the silver bracelets on her arm sang wildly. "Then I forgot."

"No problem. I was just finishing the dishes. You just missed Ryan." Kait motioned to the kitchen.

"Well, that's a shame. I think he and I ought to meet after all these years."

Kait rolled her eyes, not sure that was such a great idea.

"My, my!" Molly exclaimed, looking around. "Just look at how much you've fixed up this place already. Your grandma would be so pleased."

"Thank you. Where are you going looking so nice, Molly?"

"This old outfit? Oh, I'm just running errands. There's a sale on Dr. Pepper at Aldi's. Got to stock up." She raised a hand in a dramatic gesture. "Besides, I *had* to get out of the house. My oldest daughter and her husband are staying here for a few days. Her boys are making me crazy. Why, last night we got a call they were at Miller's Dairy Farm. In the middle of the night, mind you."

"Miller's. That's way down near the outskirts of town. What were they doing there?"

"Someone convinced them to go cow tipping."

Kait burst out laughing.

"They're city kids. They believe anything." Molly slid into a kitchen chair. "How did your talk with Ryan go?"

"It went as well as can be expected, considering I was telling the man he has an almost eight-year-old daughter."

"That good, huh?"

"Well, he seems to have burned through his anger, and now he's spending a lot of time with Jenna. And I don't know how he's doing it, either. His job is crazy."

"Good for him. Ryan Jones is an honorable man. Now what about time with you?"

"Ryan's focused on getting to know his daughter."

"I *said,* what about you? Does he know you still care for him?"

"I—"

Molly raised her palm. "Hold it right there, young lady. I've raised too many children and grandchildren not to know when someone is about to land a big fib. Maybe you want to rethink your answer."

Kait laughed.

"Kaitey, honey, if it wasn't for his mother

and your daddy, you two would be married right now."

"Molly, I don't think it's wise to try to go back."

"Nonsense. Life is all about learning from your past so you don't make the same stupid mistakes again and again, right?"

"I never thought of it that way."

Molly scoffed. "You and I both know life is short and precious. Someday you realize that all those tomorrows you put things off for are long gone."

Kait shook her head at Molly's logic, which somehow seemed to make perfect sense.

"Oh, I've got a few things for you." She pulled a freezer bag out of the paper sack on the floor. "Okra. Just stick it in the freezer."

When Kait opened the freezer, Molly exclaimed, "Braum's! I see you're getting reacclimatized to Oklahoma the right way."

"Ryan brought that."

"What did I tell you? He's courting. A man doesn't bring Braum's butter pecan unless he's courting."

Kait laughed. "You're kidding, aren't you?"

"Not hardly. Next thing you know it'll be Mazzio's Pizza."

Kait choked on another laugh. She pointed to the empty pizza box on the far counter.

"Good night, that's a man after my own heart. What a charmer. Moves straight from Braum's to Mazzio's in one day. Watch out, Kaitey-girl. Next thing you know it'll be Goldie's. He'll be proposing over burgers and homemade pickles."

"Molly!"

"I'm just saying." She dipped her hand into the bag once more, pulled out a flat white box and handed it to Kait.

"What's this?"

"Open it up. Don't you like surprises?"

"As a general rule? No." Kait removed the lid and carefully folded back the tissue paper. Inside was a framed photo of Kait's mother, Molly and a toddler.

"That's you, Kaitey."

"Oh, my goodness. Just look at my mother. Isn't she beautiful? And you, Molly—you're gorgeous. Look at your hair. It's so—"

"Black." Molly gave a disgusted huff. "I know. Don't remind me."

"Where was this picture taken?"

"Right here. On the front porch. See the window in the background?"

She was right. The photo had been taken on

the front porch of the house that had been in her family for four generations.

Molly raised her head and glanced around. "You know, I just realized that you and Jenna are the last Redbirds."

"The last of the Fields, too," Kait added softly. She sank into a chair, overwhelmed.

"What's wrong, child?"

"The For Sale sign went up today."

"Now how'd I miss that?" Molly walked to the door and looked out. "There it is, big as day."

Kait nodded.

"I can't imagine this old house belonging to a stranger," Molly mused.

"I know, but what can I do?"

Molly's hands went to her hips. "You can tell them it's not for sale. You're an Okie. Your roots are here in Granby, in this house."

"I wish it was that simple."

"It is simple. Everything that little girl needs is here, Kait. Everything you need, as well."

"I have a job. A really good job with great benefits. It's taken me years to move up the ladder in that office."

"You're going to give up a chance at happiness for a nice dental plan?"

"Molly."

"Don't Molly me. I'm guessing you're afraid,

and that just doesn't make sense. Why, you're the bravest person I know." She narrowed her eyes. "I'm also guessing you haven't chatted with the Lord about this."

"Now you sound like Ryan."

"You don't say?" She raised her brows. "But don't think I didn't notice that you didn't answer the question."

"I'm afraid of what the answer might be if I pray."

Molly laughed, then got serious. "Kaitey, God didn't give you that fear."

"I know, but—"

"*But?* But has got to be the sorriest word in the English language. You talk to God tonight and chase that fear out right now. It's useless, just like one of those pesky garden snakes that like to hide in the flower beds. You hear me?"

"Yes, ma'am."

Molly reached over and gave her another hug. "Honey, it's all going to work out. You have to trust that the good Lord who brought you back here isn't going to leave you until He's finished with what He's doing."

Kait took a deep breath. Deep down inside she knew Molly was right. But that didn't make it any easier to turn things over to the Lord.

Coming back to Oklahoma had been a huge leap of faith. She didn't know if she had any more of those steps left in her.

Chapter Nine

Kait finished applying the first coat of gray paint to the porch railing just as the postman parked his truck at the curb and walked up the drive.

"Morning, ma'am."

She raised her brush in a salute of acknowledgment.

"You must be the new resident." He glanced down at the mail in his hand.

Wiping her hands on a rag, she accepted the proffered junk mail. "That's me. Resident."

"Done a lot of work on the place," the carrier said, with a quick glance around.

"Yes," she agreed. A *lot* of work.

"I always thought all this place needed was a little sprucing up. Why, with those holly bushes trimmed back you can really see the house. Looks mighty nice."

"Thanks." Pride welled inside Kait. The place was returning to its former glory. Molly was right. Her grandmother would have been pleased.

The mail carrier nodded toward the sign on the lawn. "So you're fixin' to sell the place, huh?"

"Unfortunately, yes. I live back East."

"Tough market. But that's a fine house. Needs some work but still a fine house."

Kait nodded.

"Are you by chance kin to Jack Field?"

Kait stiffened. "Jack was my father."

The man jerked back in surprise. He looked her up and down. "Naw. Really? You don't look much like him."

"I guess I look like my mother. She was part Native American."

"Guess so." He scratched his head and adjusted his mailbag. "Funny—Jack never mentioned he had a daughter."

"So you knew my father?" Kait blinked, as much surprised as she was eager for any news to connect her father and the last years of his life.

The carrier gave a quick shrug. "As well as I know all my customers. I've had this particular route for about a year and a half. Your father would always offer me a glass of tea. To tell you the truth, I looked forward to yammering with Old Jack."

Yammering? She couldn't even remember a full conversation with her father, much less yammering. Were they talking about the same Jack Field? She hadn't even heard a pleasant word from her father since her mother died. The most she'd gotten from him in the final months before she'd left town were a grunt and a few terse, angry epithets she preferred to forget.

"I never did believe those stories about him." The postman cocked his head. "Jack was sober the entire time I knew him. Quit drinking about eighteen months before he passed. Told me more than once that he was a new man. None of my business, but he told me his liver was failing."

Kait stared ahead, regret and confusion swirling through her mind. It was as though he was talking about a stranger. She wasn't going to refute his words. There was at least some comfort in knowing that her father had apparently had some sort of epiphany in the months before his death. Had the man her mother fell in love with, the gentle father of her childhood, returned?

Finally the postman frowned and shook his head. "My condolences for your loss, ma'am."

"Thank you."

"Well, I've got to keep moving. If Mrs. Brown doesn't get her mail by noon she starts calling the main office." He gave a quick nod. "Nice to meet you, Kait Field."

Kait smiled. "Thank you. And I appreciate the kind words about my father," she responded, meaning every word.

"Nothing but the truth, you know." He gave a short nod. "You have a good day now."

Kait sat at the kitchen table staring beyond the paperwork spread in front of her. Everything was stacked in neat little piles waiting for her attention. She couldn't focus tonight, though she'd been sitting for what seemed like hours.

Too many decisions to make. Why did it seem as though she'd been the designated adult in her life for way too long? She glanced around, frustrated; maybe this would be a good time to clean the oven.

A sound caused her to lift her head. She listened. Was Jenna talking in her sleep again? She did that on occasion when she had a lot on her mind. Kait released a smile. Kait cleaned when stressed, and Jenna talked in her sleep. What a pair they were.

Kait put down her paperwork and walked slowly up the stairs and down the hall to check on Jenna. With her palm on the jam, she peeked into the darkened room. Jenna was asleep with Kitty at the foot of her bed. The animal perked her ears and meowed, as if to say all was well and she was on duty, before curling back into a tight ball.

"Take good care of her, Kitty."

Kait backed out of the room, leaving the door ajar a few inches. Moving down the hall, she paused outside her father's room. She stared at the smooth wood of the five-panel door. With one hand on the cool crystal knob, she froze and then swallowed.

Despite their falling out, somehow she always thought he'd be there. Gruff and stoical, negative and bitter, he was still her father, and she had naively assumed there would always be time to fix things between them.

She'd been wrong.

Then she remembered the postman's words. Had her father really changed?

A nudge from deep within insisted she enter his room.

Kait turned the knob, then hesitated once more before finally trying the door. The wood held tight to the frame. She pushed, finally stumbling into the darkened room. Her hands moved along the wall, searching for a switch, turning on both the ceiling fan and overhead light. The fan came to life, but the lightbulb merely glowed and sizzled before burning out.

She entered anyhow before she lost her nerve.

A small, solitary battered leather suitcase stood just inside the threshold. She stopped, staggered by the sight.

The bag was a silent accusation. Her father's last trip to the V.A. hospital. *Alone.*

"Daddy, I'm so sorry." Her lips trembled. He should have never been alone. That shouldn't have happened. But in his mind, his daughter had crossed the line and he couldn't forgive her.

Jack Field had paid the price.

Kait swallowed and carefully skirted the bag to enter the room. Nothing had changed. The shades were still drawn, the way he liked them, blocking out the cheery sunlight. On his high-boy bureau, a slightly tarnished, silver-framed picture of her mother greeted the world. Her mother's smile brought the only light into the dark shadows of the bedroom.

Kait's eyes blurred with moisture.

The same huge king-size bed dominated the room. She ran her hand along the unfamiliar navy-and-burgundy-patterned comforter. Several large matching shams were propped at the cherry headboard.

The bed linens were crisp, with creases, as though they'd just come out of the package. She frowned, staring at the bed for long minutes. Had her father done that? Had he realized he wasn't coming home? Who had brought home his suitcase? Molly?

The tidy room, however, offered no further surprises and no further answers. Jack had always been neat and orderly. Sparse. His military background and middle-class work ethic had made him a black-and-white man.

It was those gray areas that he couldn't deal with. And life offered Jack Field far more gray than he was prepared to handle. A wife with a terminal diagnosis. A child who dared to rebel against his harsh rules and dictates in the worst possible way. Abandoned and disappointed by loved ones. Yes, she could relate to her father's pain.

Kait pulled open his closet. Everything was the same. His worn bomber jacket hung in the same spot it always had. She smiled and turned her face to the soft smooth leather and inhaled.

Peppermint and tobacco.

Peppermints were always stashed in his pockets so no one would guess he'd snuck outside for a smoke. He thought no one knew.

A sad smile slipped out at the thought. She wiped her eyes and closed the closet door.

Sliding off her shoes, Kait sat on the bed, then slowly reclined. She reached for one of the big shams and a slip-covered pillow and propped them beneath her head.

Her gaze followed the rhythmic movement of the ceiling fan in the semidarkness. Circle after circle. Over and over again. She stared into the past for the longest time, reliving scenes from her childhood, eventually moving to the present again.

Everything was so mixed up. Nothing was going the way she thought it would.

Nothing.

From the moment she had set foot in Oklahoma and run into Ryan Jones, nothing had gone according to plan.

Turning slightly, she adjusted the pillow beneath her head and bumped into a solid object tucked under the covers. She yanked back the comforter and dug beneath the sheet.

A Bible?

Jack Field kept a Bible?

She reached to the bedside table and pulled the small chain on the lamp.

The black-leather volume was familiar. She opened to the front and read the inscription. It was her mother's Bible. Her father often said he had little use for their God. Kait ran a hand over the gently worn cover.

Papers were stuffed in the back of the Bible, and the rough edges of a photograph stuck out of the middle. Kait turned first to the back of the book and slowly examined every single piece of paper. Christmas cards. School pictures. All the letters and photos she had sent him the past eight years.

She flipped pages, smoothing the center pages where a picture of her and Jenna had been stuck, like a bookmark. It wasn't a picture she'd sent him. Molly must have given him the photo after one of her trips to Philly.

And yet her father had obviously been the one to stick the photo in the center of the Bible and place the book beneath his pillow.

Had he made peace with his past also? Had he forgiven her?

Kait didn't realize she was crying until a drop of moisture landed on the pages. She wiped at the spot with the pad of her finger. Glancing down, she blinked and read the words where her finger had stopped.

I sought the Lord, and he answered me and delivered me from all my fears.

"Oh, Lord, thank You for taking care of my father."

Ryan loped up the porch steps of the Field house two at a time. Someone was snoring, the sound barely audible above the noises of the night.

Frowning, he stepped onto the smooth planks of the front porch and looked around.

Kait was asleep in the glider.

"Kait?"

Her eyelids flickered, and she stared up at him, all soft and tousled. When she released a sleepy little smile, his heart caught.

"Hmm," she mumbled, though she still wasn't fully awake even as she tried to pretend differently.

He held back a laugh. "Are you planning to spend the night on the porch?"

"Mmm. No. I must have fallen asleep."

"Looks like it." He leaned back against the railing, enjoying himself. She'd be awake here in a second, and they'd go back to being wary with each other again. For a minute, he'd just pretend things were like they used to be. It couldn't hurt to pretend a little, could it?

Kait scooted up in the swing, pulling the bright multicolored afghan with her and then glanced around. "What time is it?"

"Little after ten."

She rubbed her eyes.

"You were snoring."

"I don't snore."

Then he did laugh.

Her gaze met his and she frowned. "You probably shouldn't be leaning against that railing."

"Why not?"

"I just finished the second coat an hour ago."

He sprang from the wooden rail and looked over his shoulder.

Kait laughed like that was the funniest thing she'd heard in forever. He hadn't heard her laugh like that in so long that he just stared, delighted at the sound.

"Turn around so I can see the damage," she said.

"Do I look like I just rode into town on a green saddle? No way. This is downright embarrassing. I can see from the pattern on that railing that I left a little bit of me behind."

"Is that a pun?"

Ryan rubbed the backside of his Wrangler jeans with his palms. "Think it's safe to sit on the swing with you?"

She nodded and tucked the wool blanket protectively around her lap.

"You just left the clinic?"

"Closed on time, but I was trying to get some paperwork done and get supplies ordered."

"You certainly keep some crazy hours. Ryan Jones, you need some boundaries."

"Tell me about it."

If only she knew the truth of the matter. Things were only getting crazier as he tried to sneak visits to Kait and Jenna into his insane schedule.

"I…" When she turned toward him, he stopped midsentence. The words just disappeared as he gazed at her. The yellow bug light from the porch cast a soft halolike glow upon the dark hair framing her face. He was mesmerized.

She cocked her head. "You were saying?"

"I guess I forgot what I was saying."

He relaxed and stretched his arm along the back of the swing. Kait tensed a bit before she finally decided to relax. As she did, the afghan slid to the ground. They both reached for the swatch of wool, hands connecting in slow motion.

Flustered, she accepted the afghan from him.

Silence stretched before she finally spoke. "So were you just in the neighborhood?"

"Not exactly. I drove around for a bit trying to get the courage to stop and see if you were up."

"Really?"

"'Fraid so."

"I find it hard to believe you have to gather courage for anything."

"I'm human, Kait."

She knit her brows together as she considered his words. "What's on your mind?"

"I'm a little embarrassed to ask, but Chris reminded me of something today. Actually nagged me as usual is more like it."

"Chris?"

"My vet tech."

Kait nodded.

"Will Sullivan's wedding is coming up in less than two weeks." He stared at the ceiling for a moment, trying to focus. "I know this is really short notice, but well, I'm the best man and so naturally I have to go."

"Naturally."

Ryan met her eyes. She wasn't going to give him an inch of rope to save himself. He swallowed.

"I'd be honored if you'd be my…my date. You and Jenna, that is."

"We'd love to."

His head spun toward her. "Whoa. That was way too easy."

Kait laughed. "Was it? I'm sorry. Women love weddings. We get to dress up. We get to dance. We get to eat cake. Everyone is happy. It's a win-win. Next time, ask me something hard, and I promise to say no."

"I'll remember that." Pleasure soared through him at her answer, but he tamped down the emotion. Instead, he simply shook his head in calm acknowledgment.

Kait was like a skittish horse. He'd learned that it was best to just let them get comfortable with you first. Eventually they'd trust you and let down their defenses enough for you to get close.

Timing was everything, and he had just wrangled his first date with Kait in eight years.

Not too bad for an old cowboy.

"So how come you're out here on the porch sleeping?"

She took a deep breath, and when her misty eyes met his, he could tell she was fighting her fears.

"What's wrong, Kait?"

"Just a lot on my mind the past few days. More to deal with than I expected."

"Gramps says the quickest way to untangle a problem is prayer."

"As usual, Gramps is right."

"So let's pray." He didn't wait for an answer but took her small capable hands in his. He bowed his head.

"Lord, we come to You asking for guidance for Kait as she prepares to make many important decisions. Help her to hear You amidst the noise around her. Take care of her and Jenna, and help them to find Your perfect will for them. Amen."

Head up, his gaze met hers.

"Thank you," she said softly. "I haven't had anyone pray for me in a long time."

"I consider it a privilege to pray for a friend."

Ryan rocked the swing with his booted foot and enjoyed the silence of the night and the rightness of being with Kait.

"So tell me what's got you so upset today."

She shrugged. "I had a chat with my father, so to speak."

"I'm sorry. That couldn't have been easy."

"No, but it was time."

"Family is important, no matter how crazy they make us."

"You're right."

"Have you thought any more about Gramps's party?"

Once again Kait tensed, her face anxious as she opened her mouth.

Ryan gently placed two fingers against her mouth, stilling her lips. Her dark eyes rounded at the contact.

"I wasn't looking for an answer right this minute," he whispered.

Kait continued to stare at him, her lower lip slightly wobbly when he removed his fingers. "Aw, you look like someone stole your favorite horse. Come here." He moved his arm to wrap it around her slim shoulders.

"I don't think…"

"Kait, you think too much. Sometimes a person just needs a hug. Simple as that."

They sat motionless. When he heard her release the breath of air she'd been holding in, it seemed only natural to rest his chin on the top of her head.

"That may be," she said. "But I still don't think—"

"What did I just say? Ever notice you tend to be an overthinker?"

"I am not."

"Yeah. You are."

When she didn't answer, he kept talking. "Tonight I found out I have a date to Will Sullivan's wedding with the two prettiest gals in Granby. I'm sorry I brought up the party. Let's save that for another time. Okay?"

Kait nodded and settled against his chest.

She fit perfectly.

Chapter Ten

"You're dripping paint on the floor, Momma."

Kait glanced down at the kitchen floor and nearly giggled out loud at the sight. Yes, Jenna was right. She'd been daydreaming about last night's chat with Ryan instead of focusing on the task at hand.

Too many lonely years had slipped by since she had been simply held and comforted.

Now she knew what she'd been missing. Strong arms that let her know she wasn't alone in the world. The comforting, familiar smell of a clean shirt and man's cologne as her nose pressed into his chest. The soft, warm whisper of a sympathetic word in her ear.

Yes, there was a lot to be said for showing someone you care.

And when it was one Ryan Jones doing the caring, an amazing thing happened. A feminine excitement bubbled up within her.

She wasn't sure at all how to handle what she was feeling. It was all so familiar, and yet everything was different this time.

"Momma. The paint almost landed right on my head."

Kait looked down at the large globs of white paint staring at her from the middle of the oak floor. "Are you sure Kitty didn't do that?"

"I saw it drip from that thing in your hand."

Seeing Jenna's concern, Kait tried not to laugh at the absurdity of the situation. She was having romantic daydreams like a teenager. How ridiculous was that?

"This thing is a roller, Jenna."

"A roller."

"Yes."

Kait climbed down from the ladder and wiped the spots, then scrubbed the area with soap and water, before spreading even more newspapers on the floor.

"You probably should take Kitty to your room unless you want a polka-dot cat."

Jenna looked at her mother and giggled. "Okay."

"Oh, and Jen, I left my old jewelry box on your bed. I found it in the attic. You can have it. Throw out what you don't want."

The little girl's dark eyes rounded. "Oh, thank you, Momma."

"And don't forget, we have to get those tests finished and mailed to your teacher tomorrow, so you have to study."

"I will." Jenna carefully scooped her cat off the floor and rushed out of the kitchen and through the parlor.

Climbing back up the ladder, Kait dipped the roller in the paint once again and sloshed it back and forth along the pan as she eyed the ceiling.

"Painting, huh?"

She jumped then whirled around, splattering white paint, like rain drops, everywhere.

"Nice," Ryan said. He stood behind the screen door assessing her.

"You scared me."

"Are you saying I'm scary? Because it seems you're the only woman I have that effect on."

"What effect do you have on other women?"

Ryan's brow raised as he considered her question. "Oh, the usual, I 'spose." He shrugged. "You know. Swooning and stuff."

"Right." Kait coughed loudly at his bold declaration.

Oh, she believed it all right, but there was no need to let him know. After all, it was a given that a single, handsome, smooth-talking cowboy vet was a draw to every woman in Granby. The thought was sobering.

"Want some help?" He opened the screen and stepped inside.

"You can paint, too?"

"I've done my share."

"Exactly how many kitchens have you painted?"

"Two or three."

"Only two or three?"

Ryan frowned. "How many have you painted?"

"This is my first."

"That would explain your nose."

Kait rubbed at her face.

"You just smeared it all over the place." He grabbed a rag from the counter and moistened the corner under the kitchen tap. "Come on down here."

Kait set the roller in the tray and climbed back down the ladder again. She reached for the cloth in his hand, but Ryan held it high in the air, out of her grasp.

"I can see your nose, and you can't."

"I'm quite familiar with my own nose, thank you." She tried for the rag once more.

"So you say." Ryan gently held her hand at her side and began to swipe at the spots on her forehead. "Good thing this color flatters you, because you've got it pretty much everywhere."

"Oh, you're exaggerating."

"Close your eyes. You even have a few speckles on your eyelids."

Kait didn't remember Ryan being this bossy when they were kids. She closed her eyes. When she opened them, Ryan hovered above her. She could see a tiny white scar on his right cheek where he'd fallen off a horse when he was Jenna's age.

Her glance went to his nose, with its light dusting of freckles, and then to his mouth. His smooth, full lips were mere inches away.

Kait swallowed. When she looked up he wasn't smiling, but his face was intent as his gaze slowly explored her face, settling on her own mouth.

She sucked in a breath and stepped back. Collecting herself was more than an effort. "What are you doing here in the middle of the day?"

Ryan rubbed his chin and shook his head. "Chris sent me."

"He did?"

"Yep."

"That's not good."

"So Chris had this idea." Ryan sounded slightly annoyed as he shoved his hands in his pockets and stared at his boots. "I told him you'd never go for it, but he won't let go when he gets a wild hair."

"And?"

"And I had to come and ask you straight away

because I couldn't take another second of his big mouth going on and on."

"What idea?" She held back a laugh.

"What do you think about helping out just a little bit at the clinic until we can find the right fit for that front desk and the back office?"

"Me? But you said yourself I don't even have enough time to get this house ready."

"I figured with you helping a bit at the office I could get out of there quicker and get over here to work on the house." Ryan took off his hat and then put it back on, pushing it to the back of his head, looking sheepish. "Truth is, Chris said I had two choices. I could either cowboy up or lie there and bleed."

Kait's brows rose.

"Then he ticked me off by spouting how maybe he better be the one to ask you 'cause I obviously can relate to animals better than people."

"I can see how your back was up against the wall." Her lips twitched.

"I'm glad you're finding the humor in this."

"Well, you have to admit, it is sort of funny."

"Not from the horse I'm sitting on it isn't."

"How do you and Chris even know I can do the job?" Kait returned.

"I told him you ran a medical office in Philly."

"You were talking about me?"

Ryan immediately froze, eyes rounded. He swallowed. "Look here, Kait, I have a perfectly good explanation."

"Go ahead."

He nodded and tilted his head, his attention now focused on the space to the right of her head. "Chris asked me why I keep sneaking out of the clinic."

She frowned, not sure where this story was going.

"So I told him."

"Told him what?"

"I guess I might have mentioned that you were my high-school sweetheart way back in the day."

"High-school sweetheart?" Kait paused, flattered and embarrassed by the term.

"Well, yeah."

"I haven't heard that phrase in quite a while."

"It's right up there with unrequited love, crying in your beer and your horse being your best friend. You're in Oklahoma now, Kait."

A laugh welled up and burst out in spite of her good intentions.

Ryan narrowed his eyes. "Is that a yes?"

"What about Jenna?"

"It's only for a few hours a day. Maybe your friend Molly could help with Jenna?"

"I don't know."

"Kait, I'll be straight with you. I might not be in business in a few weeks if I don't do something fast."

He released a breath. "This is totally a mixed blessing. My own practice, but I'm not so sure I'm equipped to handle it."

Kait listened as he continued to pour out his heart.

"All my time, money and energy have been on taking over the practice. I didn't have time to plan for this. Doc Hammond up and retired unexpectedly, and that meant his wife retired, too. She ran the office. A regular one-woman organizational machine. Doc's wife took care of everything from the copy machine to the electric bill. It's been Chris and me and a steady stream of incompetent receptionists since then. Even the fish have started to complain."

"The fish?"

"Apparently Missus Hammond took care of the fish tank, too."

"But I don't know anything about fish."

"You're a fast learner, too. It runs in the family."

She made a noise of concern.

"Please, Kait. I'm bleeding."

How could so few words tug so strongly on her heart strings? The fact was, she owed Ryan a lot. It would have cost her a small fortune to pay for all the repair work he'd done around the house.

She looked at him. "A couple of hours a day, right?"

Ryan brightened and he nodded.

"I guess that will work."

"If I could just get you to look at the billing, insurance and payroll, I'll be able to start sleeping at night again."

"I don't see how you've handled being so short staffed."

"It's been crazy. Once you hire a receptionist, we'll at least be treading water."

"You want me to hire the receptionist, too?"

He raised his palms. "Someone has to and Chris says I couldn't smell a goat in a flock of sheep."

"That's a little harsh. You're just too good-natured."

"Why, Kait, that's the nicest thing you've said to me since you got back."

She ignored the comment. "What if you don't like my management style?"

"You have a management style?"

"Well, yes, of course. But I imagine we can sit down and discuss it later."

"Sure, but I'm thinking anything has to be better than my management style."

"And what's that?"

"Complete chaos."

Kait opened the clinic door. A short, muscular man in navy scrubs was now behind the desk. He looked up at her and smiled, his grin warm and welcoming.

"Chris?" she asked.

"That's me."

"I'm Kait Field."

He came around the counter and offered her a handshake. "Thank You, God, for answered prayer."

Kait smiled back as she shook his hand. "So what would you like me to do?"

"If you could just check our patrons in and answer the phone to start."

"I can do that."

"You've had a little office experience, I hear."

"I have." Kait glanced at the computer then back at Chris.

"Think you can handle the computer?"

"I'm actually quite good with computers."

"That'll be a nice change of pace. I've had a few who thought I was talking about small rodents when I mentioned the mouse."

Kait laughed.

"You think I'm kidding, but I'm not."

She tried to keep a straight face. "I'm so sorry."

"Me, too." Chris grinned and reached for some papers on the counter. "I typed up a little how-to for the computer scheduling system. Pretty simple Windows-based program."

Kait nodded and examined the papers he handed her.

"Oh, and in the off chance things are slow, there's a pile of files over on the cabinet. They all need new progress notes added, and then they can be filed."

"Okay."

"And if anyone calls with an emergency, press 1 for the back room and let us know you need a triage."

"All right."

"Oh, and we have a guard cat." He pointed to a corner chair where a black cat slept peacefully on an electric heating pad. "That's Sheba."

At the mention of her name, the cat opened one golden eye, assessed the situation and fell back asleep.

"Is she sick?"

"No. Her owner moved to a retirement village in Florida and couldn't take her along."

"Poor thing."

Chris nodded. "Um, you aren't afraid of big dogs, are you?"

"How big?"

"Depends on the day." He chuckled and reached under the counter. "Canned air. Use it if necessary. Just don't actually aim for them. The sound alone does the trick."

Kait slid off her sweater and rolled it up, placing it and her purse under the counter.

"It can get a little hairy out here at times. But I guess you don't learn much if everything goes right."

She smiled. "True."

"Holler real loud if you need me."

"Oh, don't worry. I'm an excellent hollerer." Chris chuckled.

The moment he disappeared into the exam area, the phone began to ring. And ring.

"You want to cancel today's appointment and reschedule for tomorrow at the same time? All right." Kait pulled up the appointment program on the computer. "Excuse me a moment, the computer is a little slow. There now, I've got you in tomorrow's slot."

There was no point putting the receiver down; she simply pushed the button for the next incoming call.

Over and over.

"Hours of operation?" Kait frantically searched for something that listed the office hours. "Um, just a moment." She ran to the front door and outside to read the sign posted on the window. "Monday through Saturday, eight to five. Walk-ins welcome. Open Sunday by appointment only."

Good grief, Chris was right. How could Ryan possibly have a life if the clinic was this busy? Now she felt guilty for all the hours she and Jenna had taken him away from work lately.

The moment the phones stopped, the door to the clinic opened. An elderly woman struggled with the door and the animal in her arms.

Kait quickly moved from behind the desk to assist her. The large, chocolate-colored dog in her arms appeared lifeless.

"You're new, aren't you?" the woman said, her voice eerily calm as she smiled up at Kait.

"Yes. I guess I am. I'm Kait."

"This is Barnaby, and I'm Mabel."

"Hello."

"Do you think Barnaby will be in heaven when I get there?"

Kait blinked, fighting panic as she calculated how she would keep her hand on the woman and reach the office phone to dial the back room.

"I hope so, Mabel." She guided Mabel toward a chair, silently praying for Chris or Ryan to open the door from the exam area.

"My husband brought me Barnaby. Oh, that's what he said. A present for me, but I knew he

was as crazy about that little puppy as I was."
Mabel rubbed the big dog's head as gently as if
he were a sleeping child.

The door behind the reception desk swung
open, and Ryan's gaze met Kait's. He did a
double take as he moved quickly into the waiting room and knelt beside Mabel.

"Ah, Barnaby, old buddy." Ryan released a
pained sigh, his voice tender and subdued. "We
didn't get to say goodbye."

Kait fought the tears that threatened.

With care, he slipped the dog from the old
woman's arms into his own. "Mabel, I'm going
to take Barnaby to the exam room. You stay
right here with Kait."

Kait took Mabel's small, soft hand into her
own. Ryan seemed to have a knack for the right
thing to say to people. She only hoped she could
somehow comfort Mabel.

"That dog was lost when my husband died. I
knew it wouldn't be long before he went to be
with him."

A proper response escaped her, so Kait
simply patted the hand in hers and blinked back
the moisture that again threatened to fall.

"My daughter is coming to take me to live
with her. I guess Barnaby knew that, too. He
wouldn't have liked being in an apartment."

Kait nodded as she let Mabel talk.

Ryan moved swiftly through the doors and once again knelt in front of Mabel. "Did you drive here?" His tone was soothing. Gentle. As though he were speaking to one of his animals.

"Oh, yes. Barnaby loves the car, you know."

"I remember." He nodded. "Your daughter is on her way. She'll drive you home, and we'll drop off the car later."

"That's right nice of you, Dr. Jones."

"It's what friends do, Mabel."

"Barnaby really loved you, Doc."

"We all loved the big guy."

Kait sniffed.

"Do you mind if I sit outside on your bench? The weather's so pretty this time of year."

"Let me help you." Ryan offered Mabel his arm and led her outside.

The phone rang, and Kait got up and rounded the desk to answer it. "Granby Animal Clinic. Why don't I take a message and someone will call you right back." She wrote on the pad and added the note to the growing pile on the clipboard just as Ryan walked back in. He ran a hand over his face.

"Ryan, are you okay?"

"Yeah. Losing an animal is tough, and I've known Barnaby a long time."

Kait reached out and put her hand on his. He squeezed her hand in return, and their eyes met.

"I don't know how you handle it," she said softly.

"Part of the job."

She nodded.

"Thanks for being here."

"You're welcome."

"So what do you think of my world?"

"I like it. A lot."

"Enough to want to come back and do it again?"

Kait smiled. "Sure."

"That's great. You know, we have a couple of full-time positions open. Great benefits and I've heard the boss is a real nice guy."

"But I already have a job," she reminded him.

Ryan stepped closer and narrowed his eyes. His gaze became intense. "What we have isn't necessarily what we need, Kait."

Caught off guard, she stared as he moved even closer and lowered his voice. "I don't want to waste any more time waiting around for what I need in my life."

She caught her breath just as Chris burst through the front door. "Mabel's going to be fine. Her grandkids are cheering her up."

"Thanks for handling that, Chris," Ryan said, his gaze never leaving Kait.

"How's it going out here?" Chris asked.

"Good." Kait trembled, still feeling the impact of Ryan's words. She reached for the stack of messages she'd collected. "Who do I give these to?"

"Chris gets those. I'm not allowed to return calls," Ryan said.

Chris nodded in agreement. "Time is money, and we get lots of calls from lonely folks who want to chat and update us on the bowel habits of their pets."

"Seriously?"

"Oh, yeah," Chris said. Surprise crossed his face as he scanned the open file cabinets. "Wait just a dog-eared minute. Are you telling me you filed *all* those charts?"

"Wasn't I supposed to?"

"Well, sure, but I wasn't getting my hopes up. You're the first person we've had behind the desk who could walk and chew gum at the same time. Kind of a shocker."

Kait bit her lip and cleared her throat, trying not to laugh.

"Any problems with the computer?"

"No, it's fairly simple and a little sluggish. Did you know you're almost out of hardware space? You might want to upgrade your antivirus, and if you're going to run all those video games, I suggest you get more RAM. Oh, and the printer needed toner so I changed it, but that was your last one."

"I knew it. I just knew it." He glanced back at Ryan. "I'm a pretty good judge of character, if I do say so, and this one..." Chris snapped his fingers and pointed to Kait. "She's a keeper."

Chapter Eleven

"Ryan lives here?" Jenna asked.

"I thought so." Kait assessed the mani-cured lawn and the asymmetrical line of the low-trimmed bushes. Fresh cedar chips sur-rounded the crab-apple tree in the middle of the front yard. "I must have the wrong house."

The picture-perfect brick cottage had pots of bright yellow chrysanthemums on each of the three short steps leading to a small side porch where two crisp white Adirondack chairs had been placed at an inviting angle.

"It was dark the last time I was here." Kait put the car in reverse just as Ryan appeared at the front door.

"But there's Ryan," Jenna said. "So this must be the right house."

Kait parked the car, and they both got out.

"You made it." He slung a kitchen towel over

his shoulder as he walked down the steps to meet them.

"You have flowers," Kait returned, staring at the bright blooms.

Ryan frowned. "You don't like flowers?"

"Yes. They're lovely, but I don't remember flowers the last time I was here." She assessed the porch and turned to him. "Those bushes were high and the chairs are different, too."

"It was pretty dark outside."

Kait shook her head. "Not that dark," she mumbled, unconvinced.

When Ryan cracked the front door, a large gray-and-black beast jumped up and slobbered an enthusiastic greeting in their direction.

Jenna choked out a small shriek. "Momma?"

"It's okay, Jenna," Kait soothed. "Ryan won't let his dog eat us. Will you, Ryan?"

"Jabez doesn't eat people."

"Stay behind Ryan, Jen. Just in case."

"Kait."

"I'm kidding."

"You aren't helping my case here."

She laughed.

"Good boy. Yes. Good boy, Jabez." Ryan turned his head away as he reached a hand out to clamp the dog's mouth closed. "Man, Jabez, your breath stinks. We need to brush those teeth."

"His teeth are really giant," Jenna whispered, her voice wobbly.

"Don't worry, he's a vegan."

"What's a vegan?" Jenna asked.

"He only eats vegetables. Go ahead and let him sniff you."

"Sniff me?"

Jenna stood stiffly while Ryan held the dog's front paws, allowing Jabez to sniff to his heart's content. When he was done, his big tongue reached out to liberally slobber on Jenna's hand.

"He licked me." She giggled.

"That was the lick of approval. Look how happy he is."

"We're glad to hear that. We definitely don't want Jabez unhappy, do we, Jen?"

Ryan turned to Kait. "Seriously, he's harmless."

"Uh-huh." She held Jenna's hand as they trailed behind Ryan and a barking Jabez down the short hall and into a large kitchen.

"Are you still scared, Jenna?" Ryan asked.

"Maybe, just a little."

"I'll let Jabez outside to play for now."

Ryan took the leather chew toy from the floor and tossed it outside and onto the grass. Jabez's nails clicked on the hardwood floor as he raced into the backyard.

Kait turned and inspected the kitchen in stunned surprise. The entire room, from the granite countertops, white beadboard cupboards to the checkerboard floor tiles, gleamed. "What happened? Everything is so, so…"

"What?"

"Clean."

Ryan shrugged, and shot her a lopsided grin.

"I think you might possibly be cleaner than me."

"Hey, let's not get carried away. No one is cleaner than you, Kait."

Jenna smiled at the exchange.

"Let me show you and Jenna the rest of the place."

Ryan walked back down the hall. When he flipped on the light, revealing a pristine black-and-white living room and small dining alcove that had been set for dinner, Kait gasped.

"What?"

"It's gorgeous," she said.

"You sort of saw it already."

"No, this is definitely not what I saw last time."

A red flush crept up his face.

"I guess your housekeeper is back," Kait returned.

"Uh, yeah."

"It's beautiful, Ryan. Really. I'm so impressed."

"Do not be impressed. Please. It makes me nervous."

Kait glanced at the far wall, where more of Ryan's photography was showcased above the mantel with soft spotlights. The framing matched the black-print couch and chairs and the coordinating throw pillows.

In the corner of the living room, on a small ottoman, Sheba from the clinic slept quietly.

"You brought Sheba home."

"I told her she was the office cat, but she wasn't buying it. What could I do?"

Sheba looked up at Kait and Jenna and cried.

"May I pet her?" Jenna asked.

"You better, or she won't stop crying."

Jenna stroked Sheba until she purred with contentment.

A timer went off, and Ryan started toward the kitchen. "Dinner's ready."

"What are we having?" Kait asked.

"It's a secret recipe that's been handed down from Grandma Jones."

"That's encouraging."

"How so?"

"No one died eating it so far."

Ryan cocked his head. "You're kinda funny, aren't you?"

"Am I?"

"Yeah. I like it."

Kait wandered back to the kitchen where Ryan stood digging through a drawer. "Do you want some help?" she asked.

"Can you pull the salad and the butter from the fridge and grab the pitcher of tea?"

Kait placed the salad bowl on the dining-room table and poured the tea. "Jen, honey, go wash your hands."

Ryan appeared, his hands in oven mitts, carrying a steaming casserole dish.

"Don't you need a trivet?"

"Trivet? What's a trivet?" Ryan asked.

"You know. Like a hot pad. Trivets keep the table from getting burned."

"Aw, nuts. Yeah."

Kait shook her head and headed to the kitchen. Pulling drawers, she searched. When she opened the cupboard next to the oven, a bright pink sticky note on the inside caught her eye.

Dr. Jones,
The salad is ready to go in the refrigerator. Fresh bread is in the bread box. The casserole will be done at 6:30. Don't burn it this time. And don't forget the cobbler. I put it in the laundry room so Jabez won't be able to stick his paws in it again. Press

the Start on the coffeepot, and it will brew.
Good luck. You'll need it. Lucia.

Kait barely held back the laughter that threatened to erupt. It was so sweet how hard he'd
worked to make a good impression on her and
Jenna.

"Kait? This is hot."

"Coming." She grabbed two dish towels from
the counter.

"Get lost?"

Ignoring his comment, she placed the folded
towels in the center of the table.

Ryan set the casserole down and shrugged
off the mitts, tossing them on the side buffet.
"Ladies." With a low bow and a dramatic sweep
of his arm, he pulled out their chairs one at a
time.

Ryan slid into his own chair, reached for
their hands. "Let's pray." He closed his eyes
and bowed his head. "Lord we have so much to
be thankful for. As we share this meal we ask
You to bless it to our bodies. Amen."

"Amen."

"Amen."

Kait placed her napkin on her lap while Ryan
scooped up servings of casserole for them.

"What did you say this was?" Kait asked.

He passed her the salad. "I never can remember what Grandma Jones called this."

Kait's lips trembled with suppressed amusement as she took a bite.

"What's so funny?" Ryan asked.

"Nothing."

His gaze searched the table. "I forgot the bread."

Kait stood. "I'll get it. You relax. You've been cooking all day."

"I think it's—"

"In the bread box," she finished.

"Yeah." Ryan shot her a suspicious glance.

"Tell me you didn't bake the bread, too," Kait asked when she returned with the homemade loaf.

Ryan cleared his throat. "I didn't bake the bread, too."

Minutes later he turned to Jenna. "Taste okay?"

"Ryan, the casserole is really good." Jenna scraped the last bite from her plate.

"More?"

"No, thank you, but could you give Momma the recipe for the casserole?"

"I can probably do that." Ryan took her plate with a proud grin.

Jenna looked from Kait to Ryan. "May I see Fred and Ethel and Roscoe now?"

"You bet. I have tropical fish and a cockatiel, too."

"A bird? You have a real live bird?" Jenna asked.

Ryan nodded. "He's visiting until I find him a home."

"You have a cockatiel houseguest?" Kait asked.

He smiled. "A bad-mannered houseguest. Don't put your fingers in his cage. He bites sometimes."

Jenna's eyes widened.

"Down the hall, first door on the right is my office."

"I can go by myself?"

"Well, sure."

Kait's glance followed her daughter down the hall. "That's so nice of you. You make her feel good about herself, Ryan."

"Isn't that a father's job?"

"Yes. But not every father knows that." Kait reached for her iced-tea glass. She sipped the chilled beverage and sighed. "I've missed sweet tea, too."

"What? No sweet tea in Philly?"

"Not like this."

"Hmm. You know I'm resisting the urge to

tell you all the great things we have here in Granby that you don't have in Philly."

"I appreciate your restraint."

"Tell me about your life in Philly."

"You want to know about Philly?"

"Yeah. Kait, not a day has gone by that I haven't wondered what you were doing. If you were happy."

She looked at him, but his eyes gave no clue as to what he was thinking.

"Come on. Humor me. Would you?"

"What exactly do you want to know? I love living in Philly. It's a wonderful city, lots to do. But Jenna was my life, and little girls have a limited interest in culture even if you do live in a city where America has its roots."

"You didn't date?"

She lifted a shoulder. "Occasionally someone from work set me up."

"How'd you meet the guy you were engaged to?"

"His firm is down the hall from my office. We met for lunch. Occasionally dinner. But I don't like to leave Jenna with a babysitter often. When he asked me to marry him, it seemed the next logical step. Looking back now, I realize I was so desperate for normalcy that I said yes for all the wrong reasons." She paused. "Besides, I kept purposely overlooking the fact that we had different visions for the future."

"He didn't want a ready-made family?"

She sighed. "There was that, too."

Ryan's hand open and closed. "I get a little crazy every time I think about Jenna calling someone else dad."

"I'm sorry, Ryan. You asked me. I'm not trying to hurt you."

"You're right. I did ask. So I guess I have to learn to stop asking questions I don't want to hear the answer to." His gaze met hers unflinchingly, and she inhaled at the hurt she saw.

Ryan looked away. "So, how'd you end up managing that medical office?"

"I couldn't go back to college with Jenna, so I took a few business courses at night through a technical college until I got a certification. The school placed me at the medical practice, and I worked my way up the ranks."

"You're amazing. You don't let anything get you down, do you?"

She shrugged. "There isn't any point in that, is there? God's in control. My job is to put one foot in front of the other and keep walking."

Kait glanced over, and he had leaned back in his chair, his gaze on the table as he considered each word she said.

He hadn't shaved today, and even with his

light hair there was an attractive, rugged shadow on his face. She was tempted to run her hand along the rough beard.

A shiver raced over her at the thought.

"What about you, Ryan?"

"Nothing special. After college I went to vet school. Then I hit the ground running with Doc Hammond. I haven't had much time for anything else. I haven't wanted anything else except maybe…"

"Hmm," she murmured watching his lips move.

Suddenly his eyelids raised and he turned. He gazed at her with tenderness. There was something else in the depths of those green eyes. Something she hadn't seen in a very long time.

"Except maybe?"

"Except maybe you back in my life."

She stammered. "I—I don't know what to say to that."

"You don't need to say anything. I just want to be real clear this go around."

Kait nodded, acknowledging his words.

"I'm glad we can talk," he said. "We've come a long way in just a little while, haven't we?"

"Yes. And I'm glad, too." She put her fork down and smiled.

"I almost forgot dessert," Ryan said.

"You have dessert?"

"Yep." Ryan stood and walked into the kitchen. Kait followed.

He glanced around. Frowning, he opened the refrigerator, then one by one every single cupboard. Finally he looked in the microwave.

Kait leaned against the smooth granite countertop. "Laundry room."

Ryan looked at her. "The laundry room?"

"Yes. And I turned on the coffeepot."

He scratched his head.

"By the way, who's Lucia?"

His ears reddened and he shook his head. "Busted."

Kait laughed.

"Hey, it's not funny. Do you have any idea how much work it was getting this place ready for you and Jenna to come over?"

"I'm sorry. But you know, I'm really not laughing at you…"

"Yeah, yeah. I get it," he grumbled.

"Did Lucia clean the refrigerator?"

He nodded. "Like I have time. She's been on vacation for two weeks and when she got back…man, she threw a fit when she saw what was growing in there. I had no idea she had such an expansive vocabulary."

"And the yard? You really didn't have flowers last time I was here, did you?"

Ryan flinched, the admission obviously

painful. "I hired a landscape company. It was long overdue. Took them well over four days to get things in shape. Cost me a small fortune." He shrugged. "But hey, my neighbors are real pleased, and Jabez loves the new trees they planted in the back yard."

She bit her lip again. "You did all this because we were coming over?"

"Kait, I went crazy with the house because I looked around and realized this place has just been a stop in my day. Not a home. I want my house to be a home like yours. A place you and Jenna will be comfortable in and want to visit. Often."

"That is just the sweetest thing."

"You think?" He moved closer and she could see the myriad of colors reflected in his green eyes.

She nodded.

Ryan fingered a lock of her hair, pushing it back over her shoulder. Giving in to temptation, Kait placed her hand along the side of his face. A small tremor of delight raced over her at the touch of his rough beard against the tender skin of her palm.

Ryan froze. He brought his hand up to cover hers. When he spoke, his breath was warm against her skin. "Can we start over, Kait?" he whispered.

"What do you mean?"

"You and me."

"Pretend the last eight years never happened?"

"No, I'd never wish that. Jenna is a blessing I don't want to wish away."

Her breath caught in her throat, and she melted, her knees slightly weak. "That was the perfect answer, Ryan."

"Was it?"

She nodded slowly and he moved closer.

"So what do you say?"

"You mean like *date?*"

"I'm not asking you to fly to Paris with me for the weekend. How about we start with going out for dinner sometime? Maybe over to Goldie's Patio Grill."

Her breathing became shallow with anticipation as his mouth neared hers.

"Kait?"

"I'm sorry. What was the question?"

"Dinner?"

"Sure, I guess so."

Now his lips were only a whisper away. She swallowed.

"Great. So are you ready?"

"Ready?" Kait whispered.

Ryan tilted his head, a tiny smile curving his lips.

"For cobbler?"

Kait dropped her head to his shoulder and began to laugh. When she lifted her face Ryan leaned in. His lips skimmed across hers before he planted a soft kiss on the corner of her mouth.

"Yes," she murmured. "I believe I am."

Chapter Twelve

"I want a wedding just like this one when I grow up," Jenna said. She clutched her pink purse close and wiped a fleck of dust off her shiny new Mary Janes.

"Then you better marry a cowboy, because it's not every day you get to go to a wedding in a barn."

The little girl's head bobbed with enthusiastic agreement. "But it was so beautiful that it didn't seem like a barn."

"Yes," Kait agreed. "I've never seen a barn with so many flowers and such beautiful music."

Ryan approached their table, and Kait's heart began a slow somersault. His blond curls were tamed and slicked back. In the dark tux, he was easily the most handsome man at the reception.

"Are you ladies enjoying yourselves?"

"We are," Kait said.

While the wedding was held in a large barn, magically turned into a small chapel, the reception was a catered affair in two large, sky-high tents. What seemed like a million twinkling white lights dangled from the ceiling, like stars in the Oklahoma sky, and a small band played soft romantic country tunes.

"How's your dinner?" he asked Jenna.

"Delicious." She pointed to her dish. "Look. I had filet min-something, and now I'm eating shrimp. I never had shrimp before."

Ryan raised his brows. "Wow."

He sat down in an empty chair next to Kait, his hand on the back of her chair. The simple gesture caused a shiver of awareness in her.

"Cold?" He reached for her silk shawl and carefully placed it on her shoulders.

"Thank you."

"I've introduced you to the wedding party. Is there anyone else I've forgotten?"

"I don't think so, but you don't have to worry about us," Kait said. "We're having a great time. I keep running into people I know."

"That's good, isn't it?"

"It is. Oh, and I met Rose. She's Will's mother? Or Annie's mother?"

"Rose O'Shea is a little of both. She runs

herd on pretty much everything but the horses at Sullivan Ranch," Ryan said.

"Well, she's planning to take me to lunch to give me the inside scoop on one Ryan Jones."

"Yeah. Like I'm going to let *that* happen."

"Rose calls you a regular Casanova. She said you almost stole Annie from Will."

Ryan sputtered. "That's a load of cow pies. Annie and I were just friends." He continued to protest with a shake of his head. "Don't you believe a lick of what Rose tells you."

"You're turning pink, Ryan."

"Guys don't turn pink."

Kait leaned back in her seat and reevaluated his flushing face. "Yes. It's pink."

Ryan groaned. "Look, Rose pretty much makes the best pies in three counties, but she also runs the baloney meter clear off the register. Ask Will."

Kait laughed.

He ran his finger around the collar of his shirt. "Sure is warm in here, isn't it?"

Jenna turned around in her chair. "When do they cut that big wedding cake?"

Ryan grinned. "Not nearly soon enough. First there's the speeches. Then there's dancing. Finally they cut the cake, and then there's more dancing. 'Course, since you're my favorite girl, you'll save me a dance, won't you?"

Jenna giggled and nodded.

Ryan's gaze returned to Kait. "By the way, you look amazing." His voice was a low husky murmur.

Kait glanced down at her peach silk sheath. "Jenna picked it out. I just discovered she's got very expensive taste."

"You're worth it." He leaned over and kissed her forehead gently. Now it was Kait's turn to blush beneath his heated scrutiny.

The clinking of glasses signaled the bridal party's return to the main table.

"Uh-oh. Pray for me. Someone around here thinks it's a good idea to give me a microphone." He shook his head and took off across the room.

"Who are those people at Ryan's table?" Jenna whispered.

"Well, that's Annie and Will in the middle there, of course. And Ryan is the best man. Next to him is Chris from the vet office. You remember Chris? You met him at church."

Jenna nodded.

"I don't know all the bridesmaids, but the first one is Chris's wife, Joanie. The other bridesmaids are nurse friends of Annie's."

"Isn't Annie beautiful?" Jenna breathed.

"Yes. She is."

Annie Sullivan turned to her husband as

Ryan began to speak, and the look of pure, clear love on her face brought tears to Kait's eyes.

"Are you all right, Momma?"

Kait sniffed and dabbed at her eyes with a tissue. "I am. Sometimes happiness fills you so completely that it overflows with tears. That's a good thing, Jenna."

Ryan resumed his place at the table reserved for the wedding party. He adjusted his cummerbund, took a deep breath and then gently clinked his butter knife against his crystal flute to claim the attention of the guests. All eyes turned to him, but his gaze was on Kait.

She shivered again and wrapped her shawl closer around her arms. Was it the breeze from the open tent flap, or was it Ryan's eyes upon her, his heart there for everyone to see?

"Today we are gathered to honor Annie and Will.

"Life is a short journey. If you can't spend all your time riding your horse, you may as well spend it loving well. It's not a surprise that guys have plenty of discussions about life and love. But as you probably already guessed, we don't know a darn thing about any of those topics, except maybe the horse part. Oh, and since I mentioned it, we did invite Will and Annie's horses, Okie and Annie-O, to the reception, but they declined. They don't like to dress up."

A ripple of laughter filled the room. Annie glanced at Jenna, who smiled as if she understood every word.

"Now I'm going to attempt to get serious here. It was Pastor Jameson who told us not so long ago that if you're going to love, you ought to choose the Lord's best for you, and you ought to recognize that when you fall in love, it's the good Lord who dropped that knowledge in your heart. The lesson here is that it's probably a good idea to talk to the Big Guy on occasion. And if there's one final thing I'd like to leave you with that would be to never doubt the Lord's perfect timing."

He turned to Will and Annie and smiled.

"So today please join me as we thank Him for His perfect timing in bringing together this couple. Ladies and gentlemen, please stand and let us toast Mr. and Mrs. William Sullivan II."

Lifting his glass in his right hand, Ryan waited for the guests to stand and lift theirs. He continued, "We, your friends and family who love you, toast your health, happiness and your blessed future."

With a nod, he sealed the toast by clinking his glass against Chris's. Tipping the flute to his lips, Ryan swallowed with a flourish, signaling the conclusion of his speech.

Kait lifted her glass and nodded to Jenna to

lift hers. Together they toasted the bride and groom. A cheer went up, followed by the resonating sound of spoons clinking against crystal.

Will put his hands on Annie's shoulders and gently drew his bride toward him for a kiss. Applause began just as the band struck up the chords to the first-dance song.

"Oh, Momma, wasn't that wonderful?" Jenna breathed.

"Yes, sweetie. It was absolutely perfect."

The lights in the tent dimmed, and music began in earnest.

"Now what's happening?"

"The bride and groom dance the first dance. It's very romantic."

Kait felt the warm touch of Ryan's hands on her shoulders, and she turned her head to meet his gaze as he stood behind her chair.

"That was a wonderful speech, Ryan."

"Was it? 'Cause I sure was nervous."

"I couldn't tell."

He chuckled. "Had to keep my eyes on you and Jenna to keep from passing out."

"You looked like an old pro up there."

"Yeah? I suppose it's good for me to have an outlet for my hot air on occasion."

"Did you mean what you said?"

He cocked his head toward her.

"About the Lord's best."

Ryan's eyes locked with hers. "I meant every word, Kait. I've waited a long time for His best."

Of course she knew it was just the wedding, the dreamy music, the romantic ambience of the reception, but her heart kicked against her chest, and she had to swallow the sigh that fought for release.

"Well, young lady," he addressed Jenna. "Are you ready for our dance?"

"I've never really danced before, you know, Ryan."

"That's where a good partner comes in. My mother made me take lessons at Miss Posey's School of Dance."

"Really?" Jenna asked.

"Oh, yeah. I hated it at the time, but it sure came in handy once I hit junior high." He grinned. "You know your right foot and your left foot, don't you?"

Jenna laughed. "Of course."

"Then you have it half licked already. The other half is trusting your partner." He put his face close to Jenna's. "Do you trust me?"

She gave him a solemn nod as she placed her white lace sweater on her chair.

Ryan held out his hand. "Well then, the rest is easy."

* * *

Kait was staring up at the ceiling when he approached the table. His gaze followed hers to the rotating mirror ball high in the tent that reflected the tiny hanging lights, shooting prisms of color into the tent. The entire effect was magical even to a cynical cowboy like him.

When the band struck up the chords to a slow, romantic country tune, she began to sway to the soft piano melody as it swirled around the room.

"Looks like you're ready for our dance."

Kait turned and smiled up at him. "I am. But Jenna…"

"She'll be fine. Rose said she'd keep an eye on her."

She glanced across the room where Rose O'Shea and Jenna were sharing punch and cake with Rose's sister, Ellen, and Ellen's grandchildren. "You know Rose is going to have all our secrets once they're done."

"Do we have secrets?" Ryan asked. He took her hand and led her out to the crowded dance floor.

"Not anymore," she murmured.

Her hands rested gently on his shoulders, and his settled lightly at her waist.

"So why didn't I see you out there when they were group dancing?" Kait asked.

"Are you kidding? I have a strict zero-tolerance policy when it comes to the Funky Chicken, Macarena, Electric Slide and Thriller."

"I admire your restraint."

"Besides, Miss Posey only taught ballroom dancing in her class."

She laughed.

"Are you having a good time?"

"Jenna is over the moon, you know. All this is quite romantic for a seven-year-old. It's like all her fairy tales coming true."

"What about *you,* Kait?"

She breathed slowly and stared at the small white rosebud pinned to his jacket. "I think it's lovely."

"We haven't danced in a long time."

"No," she murmured.

"I like it. We should do it more often."

"I don't know if I can handle more often."

"What do you mean?"

"I'm floating on a gossamer cloud of wedding tulle and sparkly lights. Dancing with you seems surreal."

"Surreal? To me it seems just right." He leaned in close enough to discreetly touch his lips to hers.

One little touch and he felt the sizzle down to his boots. His eyes met hers, and her dark pupils dilated.

"You shouldn't do that," she murmured.

"It was just a tiny kiss."

"But, I...I can't think straight."

Ryan widened his eyes at her response. "Is that such a bad thing?"

For moments they didn't speak, caught in a spell as he led her around the dance floor.

"Why Doctor Jones, that was a lovely speech."

"Thank you, Mrs. Ellis." Ryan gave a polite nod to an elderly woman and her husband who glided next to them on the dance floor.

"Max," he whispered to Kait.

"Max?"

"Rottweiler."

"Oh."

"You be sure to bring your wife and daughter by the restaurant after church sometime, you hear?"

"Yes, ma'am, Mrs. Ellis, I'll do that," Ryan said.

"Ryan," Kait whispered. "Why didn't you tell her we aren't married?"

"That would have been a whole lot more complicated than yes, ma'am."

"But it's not right for them to believe we're a family."

Ryan stiffened. "We are a family."

"You know what I mean."

He sighed. "Does it really matter, Kait?"

"Yes."

"Kait, I'd ask you to marry me tonight and make us what you think a real family is if I thought you'd say yes."

She stopped and nearly tripped over his feet.

"Easy there. You have to signal if you intend to stop."

"I…well, I'm not ready to get married."

He raised a brow as he fought pure irritation. "You almost married that guy in Philly."

"That was different."

"How different?"

"We'd known each other for quite some time."

"Hello? You and I have known each other for thirteen years."

Kait shook her head. "That's not what I mean," she stammered.

"What exactly do I have to do to make you think about a future with me in it?"

Kait blinked, confusion on her face, as he whirled her around on the dance floor. She opened her mouth and then closed it.

Suddenly the music stopped, and the DJ tapped the microphone. Kait slipped out of Ryan's arms and took a deep breath.

"All you single ladies gather over here. Mrs. Annie Sullivan is about to toss her bouquet. And you know what that means. Look out, fellas."

The loud groans of male voices filled the air as the DJ continued. "One of those ladies is going to be the next bride."

Jenna crossed the dance floor to her mother. "Momma, what are they doing?"

"The bride is going to throw her bouquet in the air, and all the unmarried ladies try to catch it."

"Why?"

"It's a custom. The person who catches it is supposed to be the next person to get married."

Jenna grabbed her mother's hand and tugged her toward the stage. "Come on then, Momma, you need to catch it."

"Jenna, honey, really…"

Kait's expression pleaded with Ryan to intervene.

He raised his palms. "Don't look at me. I think it's a great idea."

"Thanks a lot," she mouthed back at him.

Suddenly a drumroll began, and Jenna let go of Kait's hand. Ryan used that moment to hoist his daughter onto his shoulders far above the outstretched arms of dozens of single women who were clambering for the bouquet of white roses, daisies, baby's breath and satin ribbon that sailed through the air.

"Momma, Momma! Look, I caught it," Jenna squealed.

Kait began to laugh while the wedding guests applauded the little girl on her father's shoulders.

Delighted, Jenna buried her nose in the crisp fragrant blossoms. Then she handed it to Kait with an oversized grin.

"We caught it for you, Momma."

Ryan laughed when Kait met his gaze. "What? It was Jenna's idea."

"You two don't play fair."

"I didn't know we were supposed to," he said.

Kait inhaled the sweet bouquet and smiled up into the faces of Jenna and Ryan with their identical grins. Who would have imagined such a beautiful scene just weeks ago? The Lord had His hand upon them, and Kait's heart overflowed with joy at the realization.

Chapter Thirteen

Out the kitchen window Kait could see Ryan and Jenna on the front lawn. Today Ryan wore an O.S.U. ball cap and a faded plaid flannel shirt. He had chopped the branches of several trees he'd pruned and was tossing them into a wheelbarrow as Jenna raked autumn leaves into piles.

A moment later, Jenna began to giggle uncontrollably at something Ryan said and flopped down to the grass.

They looked like a picture-perfect postcard family. Kait caught her breath and gripped the phone tighter as the realty agent on the phone continued talking in Kait's ear. "A young newlywed couple has shown some interest in the house. They'd like to do a walk-through," the agent said.

"Today?"

"Yes. Is that a problem?"

"We haven't finished repairs."

"That's fine. This is just a showing. Who knows? If they like the house, they may make an offer as is."

"An offer?" Her stomach clenched. "The sign's only been there for a few days."

The agent paused. "I must have misunderstood. I thought you wanted to cut your ties to Oklahoma as soon as possible."

"I thought so, too." Kait swallowed. "I guess I expected to have some time to prepare myself for selling the house. Letting go. I know it's crazy, but I've been gone so long."

"I understand."

Did she really? Kait wasn't sure she understood her conflicting emotions herself.

"Do you think their interest is serious?"

"I won't know until I meet them. But I wanted to be sure this afternoon would work for you."

Kait gripped the counter. "Yes, of course. And I'm sorry if I sound confused."

"No worries. And, Kait, I do want you to know that I've been in this business long enough to know that selling a house is a huge emotional step in a person's life. People change their mind all the time. You wouldn't be the first. This is entirely your decision."

When she turned away from the window, her gaze connected with Jenna's crayon drawing of the three of them at Will and Annie's wedding. The simple picture hung on the refrigerator with magnets.

Kait touched her fingers to her lips, remembering Ryan's kiss. Had it only been three days ago? Time was passing so quickly. Saturday seemed like a dream that had happened so very long ago.

She was running out of time.

Kait released a breath. "No, I won't change my mind. I have to sell the house."

"What's wrong?" Ryan asked. It was clear from Kait's stance that something had changed from the time she'd left the front yard and gone into the house. He could almost touch the tension that radiated from her.

She handed him a glass of water and turned away.

"Nothing."

He frowned but let it go. "The pruning is pretty much done. I just have to rent a chainsaw and cut down that dead sugar maple by the curb."

Kait turned, her alarmed gaze meeting his. "Oh, not the maple."

"No?" he asked.

"You said it just needed a good pruning and some TLC and it would be fine." Her lower lip trembled as she spoke.

Ryan paused. "Okay, sure, yeah. We can do that." He lowered his voice and stepped closer, his back to Jenna. "Kait, something *is* wrong. What is it?"

She bit her lip and looked away.

"Don't blow me off. I'm not going to let it alone, so you may as well tell me."

Kait glanced toward Jenna, who concentrated on piling up the branches and sticks Ryan had just cut up. "Jen, honey, we're going to take a break on the porch."

"Okay. I'm going to finish. Ryan is giving me a dollar for every bag of leaves and sticks I fill."

Kait turned to Ryan. "You're paying her? We haven't even discussed how I'm going to pay you."

"Ease up. I don't want your money."

"Then why are you paying Jenna?"

"Hey, I might not be very good with women, but I do know a bit about kids. I was a kid once. Ninety percent of parenting is a combination of prayer and common sense."

Her eyes widened at his words. "Oh?"

"Common sense says that paying her for a job well done builds a good work ethic."

"It's taken me eight years to relax about being a parent and realize love and common sense were all I needed. You've figured it out in a couple weeks."

That admission pleased him. "I must be a fast learner like my daughter."

Kait shook her head and followed him to the swing. For a change, she chose to sit next to him. That had to be progress, he mused.

"So what's going on?" he asked.

"It's silly, really. Just a viewing on the house this afternoon. No big deal."

Her eyes said she was desperately seeking confirmation that it was indeed no big deal.

Ryan tightened his hold on the leather work gloves in his hand, feeling his life slipping away again.

"What exactly is so blasted important back there in Philly?"

Kait tensed, surprise registering on her face. "My life is there."

Ryan glanced around at the porch, the yard and finally at Jenna. "Is it? Is that really where your life is?"

"You don't understand."

"Give me a little credit, Kait. I know your heart and your head are arguing."

"All these decisions and changes—my mind

is racing. I can't sleep while trying to make the right decisions."

"Oh, I think I can relate." He released a humorless laugh.

"Can you?"

"Yeah. You and I have lived a pretty safe and uncomplicated life for eight years. We keep applauding ourselves for changing, but really, how much have we changed?" He paused. "The fact is change is outside both of our comfort zones."

She nodded.

"I guess all we can do is our prayerful best for Jenna." Ryan shrugged.

"Yes. I know you're right," Kait admitted.

"I'm done," Jenna called out in a singsong voice.

"How much do I owe you?" Ryan asked, his eyes still on Kait.

"Seven dollars and fifty cents."

"Ouch. I'll have to go to the bank to get that much money."

Jenna laughed, and the sound warmed a place deep inside of him that hadn't been warm in a very long time.

"Can we go to the bookstore, Momma?" Jenna climbed the steps to the porch and grinned, her smile expectant. "I have money in my bank, too. I'd like to buy a new book."

Kait reached out a hand to dust-scattered

pieces of wood shavings, leaves and grass from Jenna's bright blue sweater.

"Sure we can. Especially after all your hard work."

"Can Ryan come, too?"

"You have to ask Ryan, Jen. He's already taken off half his day to help us. We don't want to take advantage of his time and generosity."

Ryan chuckled. "Please, take advantage. Of course I want to come, Jenna."

Jenna clapped her hands.

"And I know a place where we can get a milkshake and a book."

"Where?" Jenna asked him.

"Steve's Sundry in Tulsa."

"What does sundry mean?"

"It means they have a little bit of everything in the store. And, boy, do they."

"I probably should let you take Jenna to the bookstore," Kait said.

"And leave you here?"

"I have to get ready for the showing."

"I'll help you, and then we can all go, even if it does sound awfully counterproductive to my plans to keep you and Jenna in Oklahoma."

"Thank you, Ryan."

Ryan shook his head, disgusted with himself. "Please, I'm a pushover. We both know it."

"You are not. You're just a very good man."

"Lot of good that's done me."

When she reached out to touch his jaw with her fingers, he turned his face into her palm, pressing a light kiss on her skin.

Kait's lashes fluttered, and a smile touched her lips. "Don't you know the good guy always wins in the end?" she whispered.

"I was hoping he would get the girl."

"You never know."

Kait crossed at the corner and turned at her block. Skirting around a bicycle in a driveway, she walked up the street. The neighborhood here had sidewalks, which was unusual, as most property in Oklahoma was green grass from house to curb. She admired the neatly trimmed lawns and festive autumn decorations on front doors she passed.

Change had come to Granby, Oklahoma. Slowly but there it was, visible in the new sub-divisions and the families with small children who had moved to the neighborhood.

When she passed the holly bushes bordering her yard, she could see Ryan sitting on her stoop, his beater truck parked in the driveway. Though she'd just seen him at the clinic a few hours ago, she still found her pulse quickening at the sight of him. He stood and smiled as she turned up the walk.

"Hey," she said.

"Hey, yourself. I've been trying to reach you."

"I left my phone at home."

"Where's Jenna?"

"Children's program at the library. I'll go back and get her in an hour." She pushed open the front door.

"More books, huh?"

"That, too. She's already finished the one she bought at Steve's yesterday."

Ryan shook his head. "Are you sure she's okay at the library?"

Kait unlocked the front door and held the screen for Ryan. "They have my contact information, and Molly is there with her grandchildren."

"How do you handle it when Jenna is away from you?"

"What do you mean?" she asked.

"How do you not worry?"

"Oh, I worry. I'll never stop worrying. I've just gotten better at hiding it."

She moved to the kitchen and he followed. "I'm going to heat up some leftovers. Want some?"

"Yeah. Thanks. That sounds good."

"Hold on. Don't say yes so fast." She flipped on the kitchen light. "It's only meatloaf."

"Your leftover meatloaf trumps my frozen pot pie any day."

Kait laughed. "That's probably true, unless Lucia is cooking." She pulled a platter from the refrigerator and stuck it in the microwave.

Ryan took the iced-tea pitcher out of the refrigerator. "Gramps called about his party Saturday."

Kait tensed, and her lips became a thin line. She straightened the papers on the counter. "Ryan, I can't go to the party."

"We don't have to stay long. It would mean a lot to Gramps."

"Maybe we could take a trip out there another day instead." She offered him a small smile, hopeful for a compromise somewhere in the situation. "Just the three of us."

"It's a party, Kait. A birthday party."

"Take Jenna. I trust you to take good care of her." She filled two glasses with ice and put them on the table.

When Ryan put his hands on her shoulders and gently turned her to face him, she trembled. The heat of his palms branded her clear through the fabric. His eyes searched hers before he spoke.

"Kait, I let you down once. That's what this is all about. I get it, but will you ever forgive me?"

She swallowed, her focus on the buttons of his blue cotton oxford shirt.

He lifted her chin with his fingers. "Please, give me another chance."

Nervous under his pleading scrutiny, Kait's hand went to her neck and the smooth silver chain.

Brow furrowed, Ryan's gaze followed her movements. "Is that...?"

His fingers slowly pulled the chain into the palm of his hand, where he carefully examined the silver promise ring with its small chip of diamond. It dangled next to her mother's wedding rings.

"You still have the promise ring." His voice was laced with awe.

Kait couldn't move. When he searched her eyes, she could barely breathe.

"Of course I do," she whispered.

"You talk a good one, but you wouldn't still have this ring if you didn't have hope, just like me." Ryan took a slow breath. "It might be buried deep inside, but it's there."

She inched away and the chain slipped from his fingers to rest against her heart. "Maybe," she admitted. "Maybe I do. But I'm not that naive girl anymore, and I can't do it again. I just can't."

"What do you mean?"

"I ran into your mother at the Realtor's office. She made it clear she wanted me to leave Oklahoma. Leave *you*. Ryan, she offered me money again. The implication was very clear."

His head jerked back at the words, and his jaw tightened.

"That's why I can't attend your grandfather's party."

Ryan shook his head.

"Nothing has changed. Your parents will never accept me."

"That's not true."

"Oh, it is. How is today different from eight years ago? Any relationship not sanctioned by your parents is sentenced to failure. They *will* make you choose." She sadly met his eyes. "And I'd always lose. Always."

Ryan leaned closer, again lifting the delicate necklace. "No, Kait, you're wrong." He took her left hand in his and pressed a kiss to her ring finger.

Kait shivered with the sweetness of the gesture.

"I know I let you down. But it won't ever happen again. And you'll never know that unless you give me a chance to prove it."

Though his steady gaze pleaded, the last bit of fear lingering in her heart held her back.

Chapter Fourteen

The first time the doorbell rang, Kait thought she'd imagined it. She was deep in the hall closet sorting through coats and shoes. The second time it rang, she smacked herself on the vacuum cleaner when she stood up.

"Ouch." She rubbed her forehead.

"Momma, I hear the doorbell," Jenna called from upstairs.

"Yes, I hear it, too. Finish your homework. I'll see who it is."

Kait brushed a layer of dust off her jeans and moved to the front door.

The man behind the screen was tall and wore an impeccable charcoal-gray suit. She frowned. He was dressed much too elegantly to be selling cookies.

"Can I help you?"

"Ms. Field, I'm Lukas Jones."

Kait cocked her head, still confused. Then her brain finally caught up and she realized who she was staring at. She grabbed the door-frame for support.

"Ryan's father."

"Yes."

"Oh, please, come in." She fumbled with the latch and held open the screen door.

"Thank you. I hope I'm not interrupting."

"No. I'm cleaning out closets." Kait wiped her hands on her ragged jeans yet again and motioned to the hall.

What was Ryan's father doing here? She'd only met the man once, and that event was a vague memory overshadowed by his wife. Was this another attempt to buy her out of town and far away from the Jones family? Anxiety knotted in her stomach.

"Are you moving?" he asked. "I saw the sign."

Her gaze slid to his face, gauging his reaction, but his expression was guarded.

"Yes. Philly is our home."

"I'm sorry to hear that. I know Ryan is hoping you'll stay." His eyes swept the stairs and the French doors that divided the living room and dining room. "And this is a great house. A shame to let it go. Has it been in your family a long time?"

"Yes, four generations."

"Are you sure you really have to sell?"

Kait found herself without a response, unsure where the conversation was headed. Finally she looked at him, her words a painful admission. "To tell you the truth, I'm not sure of anything anymore."

"Then take your time deciding, because family is important," he mused, still looking around.

"I agree. Though it seems my family tree is rapidly disappearing."

"I beg your pardon. Ryan mentioned your father passed away. I'm so sorry for your loss."

"Thank you."

"And I hope you'll forgive my intrusion. I should have called first, but I don't have your number, and then I wasn't certain what kind of reception I would get if I warned you I was coming."

Kait almost laughed at the comment, but she realized he was quite serious.

"Momma, may I have some paper? I'm going to write a letter to Grandpa Jones."

Eyes wide with surprise, Lukas Jones straightened when Jenna appeared at the top of the stairs and began to skip down the steps, her hand tapping a beat on the shiny balustrade. She wore a fuzzy red sweater and bright striped wool socks on her feet. Her dark hair was pulled back into a high ponytail.

"Hi," Jenna said as she descended the rest of the stairs. She cocked her head, inspecting their guest curiously. "I saw you in the pictures."

"The pictures?" Ryan's father looked from Jenna back to Kait.

"You're in Grandpa Jones's picture album. I saw it at the farm."

"Oh, yes. I remember that huge photo book of my father's."

Jenna's eyes brightened with excitement as she connected the family dots. "You're my daddy's daddy. And you're Aunt Maddie's daddy, too."

"That's right," Lukas returned.

"You're my grandpa."

"Jenna," Kait interjected, embarrassment sweeping over her. This was going to get awkward.

"It's all right," Lukas said, with a pleased chuckle. "She's absolutely correct."

Jenna frowned, her lips pursed in thought. "But what should I call you, since I already have a Grandpa Jones?"

"How about Grandpa Lukas?"

The little girl nodded, delight brightening her face. Kait observed the conversation in stunned silence.

"When will I meet Grandma Jones?"

"Grandma Jones?" Lukas suddenly laughed,

his green eyes sparking like his son's and his father's. "She likes to be called Grandmother."

"Grandmother." Jenna savored the word. "I've never had a grandmother. Momma's mother is in heaven, you know."

"Jenna, honey, we discussed this. Soon."

"Your mother is right. I promise you. You'll meet your grandmother very, very soon."

Kait quickly moved to the kitchen to retrieve paper for her Jenna. "Jen, Mr. Jones…" She stumbled, flustered. "Your grandfather and I are going to chat."

"Okay. Can I walk to the mailbox on the corner when I finish? I promised Grandpa Jones…I mean, Great-Grandpa Jones that I'd send him a letter every week."

"I'll go with you. Just tell me when you're done."

Jenna looked at her grandfather and gave a small wave. "Bye, Grandpa Lukas."

"Bye, Jenna." He smiled, his gaze following her as she skipped back up the staircase. The corner of his eyes crinkled just like Ryan's. "She's a sweet little girl."

"Thank you."

"There certainly is a resemblance to Ryan."

"Yes." Kait turned to him. "Mr. Jones, may I offer you a glass of tea?"

"Please. Lukas is just fine."

"Lukas, may I offer you tea?"

He smiled. "No, thank you. I'm on my way to an appointment, but I wanted to stop by and welcome you to the family."

Kait blinked. "I have to tell you I'm more than a little surprised. The last time I saw Mrs. Jones, she didn't exactly share your sentiments."

"I have great respect for you, Kait—even more so now that I see Jenna and what a fine job you've done raising her. The past eight years must have been very difficult."

Kait nodded and then looked away.

He took a deep breath. "In truth, I didn't know about Jenna. I didn't know about the circumstances, either. That's by no means an excuse. What I'm trying to do here is apologize. I'm asking you for your forgiveness, and I hope somehow we…we can go forward from this point."

"Your wife feels this way also?"

Pensive for a moment, he glanced up the stairwell and then back to Kait. "Elizabeth is, well, you have to understand. She's a very passionate woman. I'd say she's coming around. Change isn't easy for her."

No, change wasn't easy for any of them. And wasn't that what she'd reminded Jenna in their first hours in Oklahoma? Those were the words on her heart when she'd felt the Lord leading her back to Granby.

The Lord's timing.

"Ryan's always avoided confrontation. But this time he certainly made it clear he supports you and Jenna. He also made it clear he wouldn't let anything stand between you."

She raised her brows, surprised.

"We're parents, too, so we have as much to lose as you do. We love our son very much."

"Thank you for telling me. It means a lot."

Lukas Jones gave an emphatic nod. "I was proud of Ryan."

He pulled a business card from his wallet and handed it to Kait. "If you or Jenna need anything, please don't hesitate to contact me."

"Thank you."

"We'll see you at the birthday party Saturday, correct?"

"Well, I…"

"Please, it's a family event, and you and your daughter are family."

"You and your son are very persuasive, Lukas."

Ryan's father smiled, his green eyes crinkling at the corners. "It's the Jones charm. We get it from my father."

Kait laughed in agreement. "Then I don't see how I can refuse you. We'll be there. Thank you."

"Jenna and I would love to go to your grandfather's party, if the invitation is still open."

"Come again?" Ryan's startled gaze met hers across the restaurant table.

Kait smiled and put down the Goldie's Patio Grill menu. "Your father stopped by."

Ryan coughed and stared at her. He opened his mouth, but nothing came out. Finally he cleared his throat. "Maybe you could give me some sort of warning before you drop bombs like that."

She gave a tiny laugh at the expression on his face. "You asked. Besides, you're exaggerating. That wasn't a bomb."

"Maybe not in your world. But in my world, yeah, that definitely was. One minute we're discussing Jenna, and the next you tell me the managing partner of Jones, Kaufman & Jones, LLC made a house call."

"He's very nice."

"So I've heard."

"What does that mean?"

"It means that on the rare occasions when my father forgets he's Lukas Jones and goes back to being 'Stretch' Jones from Tishomingo, he's a great guy. Doesn't happen nearly often enough. My mother sees to that."

"Stretch?"

"There was a time before he met my mother when apparently he was close to a professional basketball career."

"Hmm. Imagine how different life would be if he'd taken that road."

"It's all about the road we pick, isn't it?"

Kait nodded. "Yes. I guess it is."

"So what did you two chat about?" He shook his head and chuckled. "Did he ask you to consider a career in the exciting legal field?"

"No."

"Well?" He shook his head. "Boy, wouldn't I have liked to be a fly on the wall?"

"Your father isn't nearly as scary as your mother, is he?"

"Depends on who you ask. My father says more with less words."

"He does." She munched on a pickle. "Formidable. That's what I'd call him. But he was very nice, and he said Jenna could call him Grandpa."

"He met Jen?" Ryan leaned back in his chair. "Well, what do you know?" He grinned. "Grandpa? Wait till my mother finds out."

"Oh?"

"I'm kidding. If he said to call him Grandpa, then he meant it. Are you going to tell me why he was there?"

"He said he came by to welcome us into the family."

Ryan blinked, obviously totally stunned. "No kidding."

"I'm not the kidder around here."

He looked into her eyes and grinned. "No, you aren't."

Kait cleared her throat. "You talked to your family."

"Who told you that?"

"Your father."

"Big mouth," Ryan muttered. He took her hand, his thumb gently moving back and forth over the smooth skin.

She shivered at the sweet contact, and her fingers curled into his.

"The fact is, I did promise I wouldn't let you down ever again and I meant it. Someday I'm going to make it up to you, Kait."

"Make it up to me?" She contemplated his words.

"Yeah, and I've already got an idea how I'm going to start."

The waitress interrupted and set tall tumblers of ice water on the table.

"I have something for you," Ryan said when she left.

Kait frowned. "You know I really don't like surprises."

"Easy there, this doesn't hurt." He pulled a brochure out of his jacket pocket and slid it across the table.

"Tulsa Community College?"

He nodded. "This is just some basic information. The course catalog and everything is online."

Kait opened the brochure and turned it over. Her glance met his. "I'm confused."

"Kait, what do you want to be when you grow up?"

"Ryan, I stopped dreaming a long time ago. Jenna is my first concern now."

"But you don't have to take care of Jenna alone anymore. It's your turn to go after your dreams."

"I don't even know what my dreams are right now."

"You had a full ride to O.S.U. You were going into elementary education—math. Are you still interested in teaching?"

"Yes, I suppose so." She paused, thinking. "How can I possibly work, take care of Jenna and go to school?"

"One class at a time. They're all online, and

I'll pay for the classes. You can do it from home in Philly."

"Oh, no. I couldn't."

"Why not? You want to spell it out for me?"

She looked at him, searching for the words to explain.

"Kait, don't let your pride stand in the way again. You've spent way too many years not thinking about tomorrow. There was a time when you and I, we couldn't stop thinking about the future. Life can be like that again."

"Can it?" She knew she sounded doubtful.

"Yeah. It can."

"But you don't need to pay for my classes."

"The way I see it, I owe you eight years of child support. Eight years of parenting. Eight years of friendship." He fiddled with his glass. "Ever since I found out Jenna was my daughter, it's been all about me. What I feel. How I hurt. What I missed."

His eyes met hers, and he reached out to touch her hand again. "That's just plain wrong thinking. This isn't about me. It's about all of us."

Kait nodded. "Let me think about it, okay?"

"Sure. But there are a few other things I want you to start thinking about, as well."

"Like what?"

"I don't want to be a long-distance father."

Kait stiffened. "What does that mean, Ryan?" She swallowed, suddenly afraid.

"Stop thinking the worst. I don't have any answers, but I know there has to be one out there."

Kait shook her head, confused.

"I don't want to miss another minute of Jenna's life. I don't want to be a dad who just sends checks."

"Okay, yes. I get that. But how are we going to…" Agitated, she pulled her hand free and gestured, palms raised.

Ryan shrugged. "Maybe I need to move to Philly."

Stunned, Kait leaned back in the booth and stared at him. "But your family?"

"They can visit."

"The clinic?"

"They have vets in Philly."

"But your animals—"

"Yeah, Jabez and my horse might have to stay here for the time being." He shrugged.

"Oh, Ryan."

"I've spent eight years going through the motions, Kait. It isn't enough anymore. And if I can't convince you there's a good reason for you to stay, then I have to consider some other alternatives."

She was silent, humbled by what he was

willing to do for her. "No, there has to be another solution."

"I'm open to one."

"Well, you were the one who reminded me that the quickest way to untangle a problem is prayer."

He nodded and flashed a grin. "Yep. Grandpa Jones's words."

"Then do that. Let's pray about this."

"Sure."

"Okay, then." She offered a weak smile. "Sometimes I feel like all I do these days is pray."

"Yes, but now we're praying together. That's a huge step in the right direction."

Kait nodded. It was so much more than just a huge step. They were praying together about their future.

Chapter Fifteen

"Jenna's really taken to the country, hasn't she?"

Kait looked up from her lemonade to Grandpa Jones as he walked up the stairs to join her on his wraparound porch. He was pretty adorable for an eighty-four-year-old man. Today being a special occasion, he wore a starched white dress shirt with his plaid suspenders, and he'd slicked down his tufts of hair.

Kait's gaze followed Harlan's to a pigtailed Jenna as she filled Buster's bowl from a large sack of dog food.

"She likes animals, too. Just like her daddy. And you know, she was a big help gathering eggs."

"Jenna gathered eggs?"

"You betcha. She's a smart girl. Maybe next visit we'll go clean the nests. And don't worry. I'll teach her how to scrub up real well after messing with the birds."

Kait smiled. She wasn't worried at all.

Grandpa Jones poured himself lemonade and motioned to Kait's glass.

"I'm fine, thank you."

"Ryan head to the gas station for ice?"

"Yes." Kait nodded. She'd been nervously glancing at the drive, hoping he'd arrive back before any of the guests.

"Which reminds me. I sure hope you like catfish."

"I love catfish."

Grandpa Jones nodded in approval. "Good. Maddie's bringing the best catfish you've ever tasted for lunch, and I've got some nice okra. Not only that, the old goat down the road sent over her apple cobbler. Going to be a real special meal today."

Kait bit her lip and fought to suppress laughter.

"Next time you come, bring your church clothes and we'll take you and Jenna to church. Have to show off my great-granddaughter. You know, those women at church gather like bees to honey when they see a man has a grandchild. And great-grandchildren? You get double points for the next generation."

Kait laughed. "I'm sure it's your natural charm."

"Naw. I'm telling you, they think a man is respectable if he has grandchildren."

"Really?"

"Yep." Harlan sipped his drink and turned to her. "Kait."

She raised her brows. "Yes?"

"Jenna hasn't met her grandparents yet, has she?"

"Ryan's father stopped by."

"Good for him." He paused. "Elizabeth giving you a go of it?"

Kait shrugged.

"Give her some time. When you're riding a high horse, it can be a mite tricky to get off gracefully." The older man's expression became stern, and he raised a crooked finger. "Just remember, you and Jenna are family. Plain and simple."

"Thank you, Harlan."

Grandpa Jones gave her an emphatic nod. "So when are you heading back East?"

"That's a good question. I'm running out of time."

"What are you going to do about Ryan?"

Momentarily taken aback, Kait paused. "Ryan?"

"He's spent too many years alone putting on a face for the world. I'd like to see my grandson happy."

"I…"

"You know he doesn't want you to leave."

Kait gave a small nod.

"Do you love him?"

Kait opened her mouth and closed it, stunned and speechless. Leave it to Grandpa Jones to cut to the chase. Not unlike his grandson.

"Ryan and I are renewing our friendship." She chose her words carefully. "I don't have any answers, Harlan. To tell you the truth, I'm not even sure I know what love is anymore."

"Seems to me you're overthinking the issue. Love ain't all that complicated."

She frowned. Once again, he sounded just like Ryan.

"That boy *is* special to me. He's got a heart a mile wide, and he needs to be loved just that much in return."

Kait swallowed hard. She agreed, but did she have the courage to try for another chance with Ryan?

"You of all people ought to know how precious life is, Kait. Don't let it slip away with nothing but regrets to place beside your pillow at night."

She cleared her throat and searched for an appropriate response. "I'm just not sure Ryan and I have enough to build a future on anymore. A lot of time has passed, and we have different lives now."

"The two of you have more than most folks. 'Sides, you both have Jenna."

She was silent.

"Kait, when your eyes meet his, what does your heart say?"

As they spoke, the familiar shiny black pickup pulled into the gravel drive. Ryan stepped out, a wide grin on his face. His straw Stetson rode on the back of his head, and he held two plastic grocery sacks in his hands. His eyes met hers, and he winked.

She drew a sharp intake of breath.

"Yep," Grandpa Jones said with a chuckle. "See there? Now that's exactly what I'm talking about. Not complicated at all, is it?"

Ryan closed the door of the truck. Kait smiled back at him, and he caught his breath. How he wished he could hold this moment forever.

She looked right at home on his grandfather's porch, relaxed and happy, her guard completely down. Her dark hair framed her face, and her eyes sparkled. This was a picture that he'd hold in his heart for the next eight years or so.

His smile faded slightly as a pristine Lincoln Navigator pulled in behind his truck.

His parents.

He sucked in a breath and prayed silently.

*Lord, give me Your words today. Help me be
the man You want me to be, the man Kait needs
me to be. Amen.*

Greeting his mother with a kiss and his father
with a handshake, he walked his parents to the
porch.

Was it his imagination, or had Kait paled
slightly? She placed her lemonade on the table
and stood, her fingers absently adjusting the
silver chain around her neck.

"Dad, you remember Kait."

"I do. Stopped by to visit her and Jenna just
this week." Lukas easily moved his long legs
up the steps to Kait and casually leaned over
to give her a hug. "Glad you were able to make
it."

Kait smiled within his embrace. Ryan's jaw
slacked. He glanced at his mother. Her eyes had
widened, her stance relaxing imperceptibly.

"Mother, you've met Kait."

"Yes," she said, with a brief nod and a tight
smile of acknowledgment to Kait.

For a moment, no one said anything. Kait
didn't know it yet, but in his mother's world that
tight smile was pretty much as good as it got.
The tension in Ryan's shoulders eased.

From across the yard, Jenna approached the
porch. "Grandpa Lukas!"

"Jenna."

She lifted her shoulders with an excited and embarrassed little shrug. Lukas Jones knelt down and offered her a welcoming grin. "May I have a kiss?" Lukas asked.

The little girl placed a small kiss on her grandfather's cheek and whispered quietly, "Can I meet my grandmother now, please?"

"Of course." Lukas took Jenna's hand in his and turned to his wife.

Kait stood very still, watching.

"Grandmother Jones, this is your grand-daughter, Jenna."

Elizabeth Delaney Jones gave a short nod at the introduction. Her glance skimmed over Jenna. Finally a brief smile escaped her lips. "Hello, Jenna."

"Aw, go on there now," Harlan said, with a touch of impatience. "That's your son's little girl. Give her a hug, why don't you?"

"Gramps," Ryan said.

His mother pressed her lips together and narrowed her eyes at Grandpa Jones. "I try not to contradict old men on their birthdays." She knelt and opened her arms to Jenna. "May I have a hug?"

This time it was Kait whose jaw dropped.

Jenna smiled shyly and moved into her grandmother's arms.

"I'm so glad to meet you. I've never had a grandmother before."

His mother's firm grasp on her emotions cracked, and her eyes became glassy. She blinked and embraced Jenna again before standing to straighten her slacks and sweater set. When she had composed herself, she looked at Ryan, assessing him carefully. "I believe she has your nose, Ryan."

"Yes, Mother. She does."

"Is Madeline here yet?" Elizabeth asked Harlan.

"On her way. Had to switch cars—Luke wouldn't let her ride in his car with the catfish. Said it would stink up his new vehicle."

Ryan laughed. "Oh, yeah, that's our Luke."

"Ryan, you gonna let that ice melt on the porch?" Grandpa Jones asked. "Kait, you want to help him with the door?"

She smiled and held open the screen. Ryan shook his head as he moved past her to the side-by-side refrigerator/freezer in the kitchen.

"What?" She tugged open the freezer compartment and rearranged the frozen packages.

"You and my dad." Ryan tossed the bags in and shut the door. "He actually hugged you."

"I told you he stopped by."

"Yeah, okay. But you didn't mention he'd become your BFF."

Kait laughed.

"Pinch me," he said.

"Excuse me?"

"I said pinch me. I'm thinking I must be dreaming, because here I am at my grandfather's place and pretty much everything is perfect."

Kait obliged, reaching out to pinch his bicep.

This time Ryan laughed, pulling Kait close. She leaned back in the circle of his arms and smiled up at him.

"Thank you, Ryan."

He raised a brow.

"For making Jenna a part of your family."

"I couldn't have orchestrated this. It's the Lord," Ryan said.

"I guess so." She lowered her voice. "His perfect timing."

"Uh-huh."

Kait closed her eyes when he bent his head and placed a light kiss upon her lips. He smiled as she breathed a soft sigh of pleasure.

"You two going to take all day?" Grandpa Jones hollered through the screen.

"No, sir, Gramps."

"Well, hurry on out here then."

"We're coming. I was just showing Kait your cookbook collection."

Harlan Jones laughed. Long and hard. "Son, I don't have no cookbook collection."

Ryan kissed Kait one last time before taking her hand and pushing the screen door open.

The heat was still I saw another, shot from gone to her camera.
You stood there trying to make
her fingers and she read them then

Chapter Sixteen

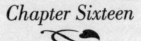

"Momma, we're home."

"Coming."

Kait grabbed a dish towel to wipe her hands and headed to the front porch to greet Jenna and Molly Springer.

She held the screen for them and took Jenna's backpack and pink sleeping bag from Molly.

"Look at you," Kait said. She ruffled Jenna's hair. "You have curls."

"Molly played beauty parlor with us. I have nail polish." Jenna held out her hands and showed off her pink-tipped fingernails.

"You're beautiful. Tell Miss Molly thank you, and then it's study time for you. You're going back to real school in a week."

"Thank you, Miss Molly. I had so much fun."

"Aw, Jenna, we loved having you."

Kait's glance followed her daughter up the

stairs. "You are such a good grandma. Tea parties, sleepovers *and* beauty parlor?"

"Well, you're only young twice, and the second time, with the grandkids, is even more fun than the first go 'round."

"Iced tea?"

"Yes, thank you. I can use a little caffeine. The kids are fun, but my giddyup doesn't get up and go as quickly as it used to."

Kait laughed as she slid the pitcher from the refrigerator.

"Jenna's all about weddings these days, isn't she?"

Kait nodded. "The Sullivan wedding was incredible."

"So I heard."

"I'll bet she gave you an earful."

"A regular news report on everyone in Granby, including her grandparents. And more than that, Jenna tells me you and Ryan are getting along very nicely." Molly raised her brows.

"Oh, no. What did she say?"

"Only that you and Ryan were dancing at the wedding, and you went to dinner the week after that."

"Jenna and I both danced with Ryan at the wedding, and as for going out, it was only hamburgers."

"Goldie's Patio Grill?"

Kait nodded.

"Oh, my. What did I tell you?"

"Molly."

"I'm just saying."

Kait narrowed her eyes. "Why are your lips twitching?"

"I'm enjoying watching you try to talk yourself out of a relationship with your daughter's daddy."

"Molly, we're working together for our daughter."

"That's very nice, but don't discount working together for each other."

Kait shook her head and sank into a chair.

"What's wrong?

"Molly, he offered to move to Philly."

The older woman's eyes widened and her lips curved into a smile of pleasure. "He's not going to let you go."

"I can't let him leave everything here...for us."

Molly reached over and took Kait's hand. "You know, Kaitey, it takes courage to let someone love you."

Kait was silent.

"I told you last time I was here that you are just about the bravest person I know. I meant that."

"I don't know that I'm as brave as you give me credit for."

Molly patted her hand. "Never you mind, you'll figure it out."

"Do you think so?"

"Oh, absolutely. It's all going to work out in God's timing."

The sound of something hitting the roof made both of their heads swivel toward the ceiling in unison.

"What was that?" Molly asked.

"I'm not sure. I hired a company to trim those really huge maples in the backyard. The ones that touch the roof. Ryan suggested it."

She pulled glasses from the cupboard and poured, pausing to wipe up a small spill with a wet cloth. "They're supposed to come back tomorrow to chip the wood."

"Then who was that I saw on the roof?"

"No one's on the roof. They've all gone home."

Molly sipped from the glass. "Sweetie, I'm telling you there's a very nice-looking young man on your roof. Very nice-looking indeed. Why, if I were a few years younger I might be tempted to invite him home for supper."

"Are you sure?"

"Am I sure I'd invite him home for supper?"

Kait struggled not to laugh. "No. Are you sure you saw someone on the roof?"

"He was much too cute to be my imagination. Besides, he waved to me and called hello to Jenna as we got out of my truck. And I know I didn't just imagine that noise on the roof, either."

Kait's eyes widened in alarm. "I told him not to get up on that roof again." She tossed the dish towel in her hand on the counter and raced out the screen door. "And it rained last night. That old roof will be slick."

"Him who?"

"Ryan."

Molly grinned. She tidied her Western blouse and smoothed back her hair. "It's about time I met your man."

"He isn't my man. And I may kill him before you get to meet him."

Kait ran to the front yard and glanced around. Sure enough, Ryan's old Ford was parked down the street.

"What are you doing, Kait?" Molly called.

"I'm going to make him get down. Right now."

Molly chuckled. "Good luck with that."

"Ryan?"

The loud noise of the leaf blower drowned out her calls, so she moved to the side of the house. This time she cupped her hands to her mouth and yelled his name.

The noise stopped and she tried again. Suddenly Ryan appeared on the side of the left dormer. He stood tall in jeans and a flannel shirt with a baseball cap on. Holding a large leaf blower like a missile launcher, he stared down at them with a big grin.

"Kait. I thought I heard your dulcet tones." He wiggled his brows. "Did you say you want me?"

Molly chuckled. Kait put her hands on her hips. "Funny, Jones. I thought we agreed you wouldn't get on the roof anymore."

He took off his hat for a moment, scratched his head and pursed his lips. "Kinda interesting how two people can hear different things in the same conversation, isn't it?"

Molly sputtered and began to laugh. "Oh, I like him. I like him a lot. He's going to give you a run for your money, Kaitey-girl."

Ryan tipped his hat to Molly. "Hello again, ma'am. Nice morning."

"Good morning. I understand you're Jenna's daddy."

"I am. Pleased to meet you."

"I'm Molly Springer."

"Ms. Springer. I've heard a lot about you."

"All good, I hope."

"Oh, yes, ma'am."

"Such a charmer," Molly whispered to Kait. "You can call me Molly," she called to Ryan.

"Ryan, please, could you come down?" Kait asked.

"Since it so happens that I'm done cleaning the gutters, I'm happy to oblige."

He disappeared to the other side of the dormer. Kait released the breath she'd been holding.

Moments later, a loud crash and a yell echoed into the morning.

"Ryan?" She took off running with Molly close behind. A metal gate stood between her and the backyard.

Muttering, she fumbled with the simple hook closure. Then kicked it.

"Kait, wait, let me get the latch." Molly unhooked the fence and stood back as Kait barreled into the yard. Tripping over the uneven stone pavers, she lost a sneaker and hit the ground.

"You okay, Kaitey?"

She nodded as she scrambled to her feet and headed into the yard.

Kait gasped at the sight of Ryan's prone body.

He slowly raised himself up on an elbow and blinked.

"Oh, Ryan," she moaned.

* * *

"Ouch, careful, that hurts."

Kait's lips formed a thin line. She applied the fresh ice pack to his ankle and adjusted the ottoman but said nothing. Jenna was in the kitchen eating lunch, and Kait didn't dare rail on Ryan until her daughter was out of earshot.

Besides, if she started, she might not be able to stop. Worst of all, she might burst into tears and collapse into his arms and admit that for one awful, awful moment she thought she'd lost him. Kait wrapped her arms around herself.

"Boy, I sure wish I had superpowers," he said.

She raised a brow.

"I'd like to know what you're thinking right now."

"Are you aware that I have been banned from the emergency room at St. Francis Hospital?"

"Naw?"

"That big blonde nurse wouldn't let me in your exam room until I got in her face."

Ryan laughed. "You? You got in her face?"

"She said only family could see you." Kait narrowed her eyes in indignation. "Why, I'm just as much family as your sister."

"'Course you are." He gave her a tender smile.

"You scared me to death," she snapped, irritation winning again.

"What? You think I did that on purpose? The cord from that leaf blower got tangled, and I lost my footing."

"You're a father now. You can't afford to be irresponsible."

"I wasn't being irresponsible. I was cleaning gutters. Fathers do that, Kait. Get used to it."

"Well, it's wrong. Plain wrong. You're lucky you slid instead of pitching over the edge."

Kait blinked as a couple other scenarios raced through her head. She touched the back of his head, gently running her fingers over his scalp. "Are you sure you didn't hit your head?"

Ryan chuckled and pulled her hand away. "I told you, that old metal awning broke my fall. 'Course I broke the awning. Just add it to my to-do list."

She rolled her eyes.

"You probably better ask for a few more weeks. I don't see how I'm going to be able to finish all those repairs on schedule now."

"I don't care about the repairs. It's you…" Kait released a loud breath of air. "Oh, never mind."

"Can't you just admit you care?" he whispered.

Kait got her face close to his. "I do care. You

know that," she whispered right back. "But this isn't about you and me."

"Sure it is."

He tucked her hair behind her ear.

"Stop that." She swatted at his fingers and moved from his reach.

Ryan grinned all the more. "Anyhow, I'll be fine. My ego's bruised plenty more than my ankle. You heard the emergency-room doctor. It's just a sprain. A week or two on crutches and I'll be able to climb the roof again, good as new."

"He said three weeks. And I didn't hear anything about roofs."

Just then Jenna wandered into the living room.

"Did you finish your lunch, Jen?" Kait asked.

She nodded, her eyes round and her lower lip quivering.

"Honey, what's wrong?"

A fat tear fell from her eyes, followed by another. She sat on the ottoman next to Ryan's outstretched leg.

"Jenna," he said. "Tell me what's wrong, darlin'." With the pad of his thumb, he caught a falling drop of moisture.

"I just found you, Ryan. I don't want anything to happen to you."

Kait swallowed, her eyes filling. Jenna had

just said everything she'd been holding in her heart. Instead she'd masked her concern with irritation. Kait turned away and wiped her eyes.

When she turned back, Ryan had pulled Jenna onto his lap and was rocking her like the little girl she was.

Kait sat on the arm of the huge stuffed chair and pushed back Ryan's blonde curls before pressing a kiss to his forehead. "Jenna's right, you know."

He nodded in agreement. "It's enough to make a fella promise to never climb another roof."

"Good, because we care about you. You have to take care of yourself. For us." Inching closer to father and daughter, Kait reached out to stroke Jenna's back. As she did, Ryan's eyes met hers.

Kait smiled. Yes, this was what being a family was all about.

Chapter Seventeen

"Ryan, will you marry us?"

"Hello?" He looked up from the checkers game. "What did you say?"

They were on Kait's porch playing the best three out of four, and Jenna was still beating the pants off him, so he supposed it really didn't matter how hard he looked at his pieces, she was still going to win.

"Will you marry us?"

"Marry who?"

"Me and Momma. I caught the bouquet, remember?"

He glanced through the tall porch windows at Kait as she prepared lunch. "I hate to say this, sweetheart, but I talked to your momma about marriage recently, and she vetoed that idea so fast my hat was spinning."

Jenna's brows knitted as she gave his answer

deep thought. A few minutes later, she shook her head. "Well you must not have done it right."

He looked at the earnest expression on her face and knew this was a serious discussion they were about to have, so he adjusted the splint on his sprained ankle, stretched his leg out on the stool and got comfortable. "Are you saying there's a right and a wrong way?"

Jenna slowly nodded.

"So you think that if I asked her to marry me the right way, she would say yes?"

"Of course." She studied the game board. "And now is a really good time."

"How's that?'

"She loved Annie and Will's wedding. I saw her crying. She told me that when you're happy, it fills you up and spills over into tears."

Kait cried. Kait never cried.

"How are you thinking we're going to work this, Jen?"

Jenna jumped his black piece then looked back up at him. She shrugged. "Sorry."

"It's okay. I'm getting used to being skunked."

"Tomorrow I'm going to Molly's house after church. We're having a tea party. So maybe that would be a good time."

Ryan scratched his head as he gave Jenna's words careful consideration, going through a dry run in his head. The idea had merit, except for the part where Kait shot him down. Maybe he could stall Jen a little while he worked on the romance part a bit more.

"But I don't have a ring."

"It's Saturday. Couldn't you go and get one today?"

He stared at Jenna, stymied. She looked like a seven-year-old, but apparently she was just a very short, wise grown-up hiding in a kid's body. "I guess I could do that. What kind of ring should I get?"

"Simple. Momma says it's not the size of your ring that counts but the size of your heart. She says a simple ring is best."

"You talked about rings?"

"Well, sort of. At the wedding I asked to see Annie's wedding ring. I asked a lot of questions. Then Momma and I were discussing rings." As if to prove her point, she continued. "Will loves Annie a lot, you know, and Annie has a simple ring."

"I see." Ryan glanced in the window again at Kait. She caught him watching and smiled— one small smile that warmed him clear from the inside out. He turned back to Jenna.

"And then you have to get down on your knee and ask her to marry you, because that's what we saw in a movie we watched the other night. Momma loves that movie."

"Good thing I have you around to help me with all this."

Jenna shook her head in agreement. "After that, you have to take her on a honeymoon. I can stay with Molly or Aunt Maddie or Gramps when you do that."

Suddenly she screwed up her face, as though she were perplexed.

"What's the matter?"

"Why do they call it a honeymoon?"

"Not sure. It's a pretty silly name, isn't it?"

She nodded and looked into his eyes, her face solemn.

"Now what are you thinking about?" he asked.

She scooted her chair closer to him and lowered her voice. "Do you think you and my momma will have lots more kids?"

"That's what's called putting the horse before the cart."

"It is?"

"First we have to see if she'll marry me." He put his hand on Jenna's. "But if I take all your suggestions and she says yes, and we do get married, well, I'd like to have lots more kids. Maybe fill up this big old house."

Jenna stared at him, considering his words.

"Of course you'd always be our favorite oldest child."

Jenna sighed with pleasure at his words.

"Okay, now, Jen, I have a question for you."

"Sure."

"Do you think you could start calling me Dad?"

She thought for a moment. "Dad. I like that."

"Me, too."

Ryan scratched his chin and glanced back into the kitchen at Kait one more time. "But I'm not sure about this getting married thing. Are you absolutely sure she's going to want to marry me?"

"Oh, yes."

"How can you tell?"

"Well, she doesn't clean nearly as much as she used to. And she's spent a lot of time just smiling kind of goofy the past few weeks. Mostly after you've been over."

"Huh. No kidding."

"Girls know these things." She paused. "Dad."

He grinned and savored the simple word.

"And besides," she continued. "I asked Miss Molly just to be sure, and she said so, too."

"Ah, exactly what did she say?"

"Miss Molly said Momma still has fear in her heart. But once she lets it go, she'll have room in her heart to be brave and marry you."

Ryan swallowed, humbled by the simple words he knew to be true. He cleared his throat, swallowing the lump of emotion that had choked him up for a moment.

"Well, it's good you gals have done all the legwork for me. Anything else I should know?"

"Flowers. Bring her flowers."

"Roses, maybe?"

"No. Momma says roses are too fancy and they die fast. She likes those big daisies."

Ryan shook his head. "I don't know what big daisies are."

Jenna looked at him like he was a few eggs shy of a dozen. "Just go to a flower shop. They'll know."

"Okay." He nodded. "Simple ring. Big daisies. Anything else?"

"Tell her you love her, of course."

He winked at Jenna. "That's the easy part."

Ryan sat in his black crew cab parked outside Kait's house, just staring at the enormous bundle of flowers on the seat.

He was a nervous wreck.

And he ought to be. He was following the detailed courting instructions of a seven-year-old. What if Kait said no? He couldn't handle another rejection. Twice in a lifetime was plenty.

What was wrong with the woman? Couldn't

she see they belonged together? He could. Jenna could. Even Molly Springer could.

But she'd let him kiss her a few times. And they were pretty good kisses, as far as kisses went.

That had to be a positive sign. Right?

Aw, nuts. Now he was talking to himself. And grasping at straws.

Annoyed with the situation in general, he brushed cat hairs off his crisp blue shirt and black Wranglers. Opening the glove box, he popped a mint in his mouth. Best to cover all his bases.

He got out of the truck and carefully closed the door so she wouldn't hear him. For minutes he simply leaned against the cab, careful to keep his weight off his ankle as he watched the house.

She'd asked him if he believed what he said about God's best at the Sullivan wedding. That sure sounded encouraging, too.

Finally he reached into the front seat for the flowers, slapped his straw Stetson on his head and half walked, half limped the long, lonely stretch to the porch.

It seemed to take hours before he was standing on the front walk and staring at the door. Taking the steps two at a time before he chickened out, he stood face-to-face with the front door. And knocked.

Ryan breathed slowly and evenly, chasing off the herd of stampeding nerves that raced across his gut.

The front door opened, and Kait smiled at him from behind the screen. That smile melted away a little more of the anxiety that had his palms sweating.

"Hey, Ryan. Did I know you were coming over?"

"Is this convenient?"

"Of course. But I'm not exactly dressed for company." She looked down at her faded jeans and college T-shirt and shrugged.

"You look like a kid."

She crinkled up her nose. "Like Jenna?"

"Better."

"Is that a good thing?"

Arrgh. Now he sounded like a babbling idiot.

"What I mean is you look beautiful."

"Good answer." She laughed. "Come on in. Where are your crutches?"

He bent down and tapped his leg. "Walking cast."

"But you're being careful, right?"

"Kait, I promised not to climb on the roof, didn't I?"

"Yes, you did."

"All right, then. That's promise enough for now."

"Have you had lunch? How about leftovers? We tried Lucia's third-generation casserole last night." She grinned. "It was delicious. Almost as good as when you made it."

He gave her a weak smile.

"And there's leftovers."

"No, thanks. I'm not real hungry." Fact was, his stomach had started doing somersaults again, and he couldn't eat if he tried.

"What do you have there?" Kait asked, staring at the hand he held behind his back.

"Oh, yeah. Sorry. I almost forgot. These are for you."

Her eyes widened at the two-fisted bunch of pastel flowers wrapped in tissue paper that he thrust at her.

She buried her nose in the blooms. "I love gerbera daisies. How did you know? This is so sweet."

Score one for Jenna.

He pulled out a kitchen chair, turned it around and sat with his arms loped over the slats.

"Wasn't that a powerful sermon this morning?" Kait asked as she searched the cupboards.

"Uh, yeah." Truth was, he'd barely heard a thing Pastor Jameson had said. He was too busy watching Kait and rehearsing his little speech. He hoped the Lord would understand this one time.

Kait turned to him. "I can't reach that vase. Do you mind?"

He stood and easily grabbed the cut-glass vase from the cupboard.

"Thank you."

"Sure thing," he mumbled.

"Ryan, are you feeling okay?" She trimmed the flower stems and turned to him.

He leaned against the counter and watched her. "I've got a lot on my mind, I guess."

"Anything I can help with?"

"Naw, this is one of those things I have to take care of myself."

Kait placed the flowers on the table and smiled. "Gosh, they're beautiful." She wiped down the counter and put the clippings in the trash.

"Kait, could you sit down?"

"Oh-kay. Are you sure you're not sick? You look a little flushed." She put her palm to his forehead, concern clouding her eyes. "Maybe you're coming down with something."

Ryan took her hand and held it for a moment before releasing it. "I'm not sick. *Yet.* And if

I'm coming down with something, it's probably fatal, so no point worrying about it anyhow."

She raised her brows.

"Please, sit down." He pulled out her chair then sat back down himself.

"Kait, we need to talk."

"Uh-oh. When I say that to Jenna, she asks if she's in trouble."

He couldn't help chuckling. "You aren't in trouble."

"That's a relief."

He folded and unfolded his hands. "Kait, what is it exactly you're looking for in a husband?"

She blinked. "That's a bit random."

"Humor me."

"I don't know that I am looking for a husband."

"Hypothetically speaking. What would you be looking for in a husband if you were looking for a husband?"

"Well, let me think for a minute." She frowned and stared at him.

Ryan shifted, uncomfortable under her scrutiny.

"Well, I don't need a man who smothers me or a man who's so involved in his own life he can't be there for me when I need him."

He wiped a droplet of water from the table-top with his finger, listening carefully to her answer. "Okay."

"Ryan, I just need you to walk beside me, all the way. No matter how hard things get. It's not unlike the Lord. Always there, even if you've got to carry me on occasion. And I'd do the same for you."

His head jerked up. "I thought we were talking hypothetically."

Her lips twitched. "Are we?"

"I don't know—you tell me."

He stared at her. He loved her so much and had for so long. More today than eight years ago, if that was even possible. Before he knew it, he'd leaned across the table until he was close enough to touch his mouth to her soft lips. He released a breath.

This was right where she belonged.

Kait's eyes were still closed when she began to talk. "Did you see the front lawn?"

"What? You mean the sugar maple? Yeah, I noticed. Won't know for sure until spring, but it looks like that tree is going to make it." He smiled.

"No, not that," Kait said. "The sign is gone."

Ryan shot up in the chair and hobbled to the door.

"You sold the house?" The air whooshed

from his lungs as he turned back to her. "Kait, you sold the house?"

"No. We're staying in Granby."

He grabbed her hand and pulled her into his arms. He nibbled from her ear to her mouth, finally settling his lips on hers with purpose.

Kait's hands wrapped around his neck and tugged him closer.

"You're staying." He murmured the precious words against her mouth. When he came up for air, he stared straight into her dark eyes.

"What made you change your mind?"

"Someone has to keep you off the roof."

Ryan laughed. "This is going to be a lot easier than I thought." He swooped down for another kiss.

But Kait was faster. She put her hand against his mouth.

"Ryan, what are you talking about?"

For a moment he stared, as if memorizing every feature. As though she might disappear again.

How he loved her. That heart-shaped face just like Jenna's, the stubborn little chin, the compassion and determination in her eyes. And that mouth—made for kissing him.

He had the rest of his life for kissing. Right now he had to slow down and do this right. Do it the way Jenna told him to.

Yeah, just the way Jenna told him.

So he took the chain from around Kait's neck, gently lifted it over her head and set it on the table. "Well, first off, you don't need this anymore."

She looked at him, confused. Ryan settled her back in the chair.

Getting down on one knee, he reached into his back pocket and took Kait's left hand in his.

"Kait Field, I've waited forever to ask you this. Will you marry me?"

Her eyes widened as she stared down at him. "You bought a ring?"

"Well, yeah, don't you like it?"

She took the ring from him and examined the marquise in the simple platinum setting. "It's absolutely lovely."

"Will you wear it?"

"You want me to—" She paused, flustered, her eyes welling up with moisture. "—To marry you?"

"I just asked you, didn't I? I love you. I love Jenna. I want us to be a family."

"Ryan, you don't need to marry me."

"Pardon me?"

"I know you're bent on paying me back for what you think life stole from me. And don't think I don't appreciate it. But you don't need to ask me to marry you."

Ryan shook his head. "Whoa. For a moment there I thought I heard you say this was a pity proposal."

Kait laughed. "That is not what I said."

"Sure enough sounded like it to me."

"Ryan, you're doing the right thing."

"What are you talking about, Kait?"

"Asking me to marry you. It's all part of do the right thing, be honorable. Ryan Jones, good guy."

He blinked. "Are you kidding me? You think I'm asking you to marry me because it's the right thing to do?"

She nodded and turned her head away.

Ryan captured her chin and turned her to face him. "Is that what you thought when I asked you about it at the Sullivan wedding?"

She nodded again.

"In a pig's eye," he growled.

"Are you sure?"

"Well, of course I'm sure. Not a day has gone by in the past eight years that I haven't loved you. You're God's best for me, Kait, and I've always known that."

A small tear rolled down her face and over her lips.

Ryan reached out a finger to catch the moisture. "Happy tears?"

She nodded, her mouth quivering with a small smile.

"Jenna told me about those."

"She's a smart little girl."

"Yes. She is. Someday I'll tell you just exactly how smart she is."

He took Kait's hand again and looked into her eyes, asking the question again, without words. When she nodded, he thought his heart would burst. Taking a deep breath, he slipped the diamond ring on her finger.

She glanced at the ring and placed her hand on his face, caressing his cheek. "Ryan, I've been fighting this...us, for so long because I was afraid."

"Afraid I'd let you down?"

"Maybe a little, and afraid that Jenna was the only thing that brought us together."

"Aw, Kait."

"I'm so ashamed of myself."

"Ashamed of yourself?"

"It took you falling off a roof for me to really get it. Suddenly I was faced with the real possibility that I could lose you. I never want to have to go there again."

Leaning forward, she kissed him, knocking his straw Stetson to the ground.

"I told you I always keep my promises, didn't I?"

"I'm counting on that."

"This is pretty much the best minute of my life," Ryan said.

Kait laughed. "Mine, too."

"You know it's not going to be easy. My family's always a challenge. But don't worry. I'll always have your back."

"God never said it was going to be easy. He said he'd never leave us."

"Yeah, and you better cling real hard to that scripture, because at some point we're going to have to do family dinner at the Hill. Luckily Helen is a really good cook, so most of the time you can just keep chewing and nodding and not actually have to talk at all."

Kait laughed.

"Then there's the question of the kids."

"The kids. What kids?" Her brows shot up.

"Our kids. I want lots of them. So is it going to be your house or mine?"

Her mouth opened to form a small O. "Isn't this a bit premature?"

"No. I've got to get a bigger fence built so Jabez doesn't get out of your yard."

"You're talking about animals."

He winked and kissed her again. "What did you think I was talking about?"

"I hoped you were talking about filling the house with lots of brothers and sisters for Jenna." She laughed. "Someday."

"There's that, too."

Kait buried her head in the crook of his neck. "Oh, Ryan. We're so fortunate to have gotten a second chance."

"Yeah, we are, and I know a whole lot of folks who are going to be really happy about it."

"All part of God's perfect timing, isn't it?"

"Amen to that."

"I love you, Ryan."

"Love you more, Kait."

Epilogue

"Momma, are we going to the livestock barn next?" Jenna asked. "Faith wants to show me the animal birthing pen."

Kait's hand moved to her rounded abdomen. "Yes. But you have to slow down. I'm waddling as fast as I can, and I can barely keep up with you and your daddy's long legs."

"Sorry, Momma."

"Where is Ryan?" Kait asked.

"He's talking to Mrs. Johnson. Her cockapoo is about ready to deliver."

"Oh, no. I smell trouble. We can't let him bring another animal home. There won't be room for the baby."

Jenna giggled.

"I'm serious, Jen."

"Oh, look, Momma, funnel cakes. May I have one?"

"Sure."

Jenna skipped up to the stand and stood beneath the striped canopy. "Eight funnel cakes, please."

"Eight, Jenna?"

Jenna counted on her fingers. "You, me and Daddy. Aunt Maddie and Faith. Uncle Luke and Grandmother and Grandpa Lukas."

Kait laughed. "Eight." Who'd have thought she'd be at the Tulsa State Fair a year later with a family of eight? She patted her stomach. Eight and a half.

She handed the vendor several bills.

"We have lots of family now." Jenna released a satisfied breath.

Ryan joined them and put his arm around his daughter. "Yes, darlin', you do. A big family. And it's getting bigger every day."

"Hey, are you talking about my belly?" Kait asked with mock indignation.

"No way. We love your belly, don't we, Jen?" Jenna giggled.

"How do you like your new name, Jenna?" Ryan asked.

"I like it."

"Jenna Field Jones. Sounds mighty impressive. Like you're famous."

Jenna smiled into her father's eyes. "Do I get to help name my baby brother?"

"Sure, we all get to name him."

The vendor began to hand Kait waxed tissues filled with funnel cakes. She passed several to her daughter. "Here you go. Bring these over to Aunt Maddie and Faith."

"Hey, let me help." Ryan took another one from Kait and followed Jenna.

When he returned to his wife's side, he chuckled.

"What's so funny?"

"You've got powdered sugar on your nose. How'd you manage that?"

He leaned close and, with the pad of his finger, wiped the white spot off her face. "Close your eyes, you've got some on your lids."

Kait closed her eyes. Gently he wiped the sugar from her eyelids. When she opened her eyes, he leaned in and tenderly placed his lips on hers.

"I love you, Kait Jones," he said.

"Keep telling me."

"I promise I'll tell you every single day for the rest of our lives."

She sighed. "That's a promise I can live with."

* * * * *

Dear Reader,

Thank you for reading Ryan and Kait's story. Ryan Jones was a secondary character from my first Love Inspired release, *The Rancher's Reunion*. Ryan is such a bigger-than-life character that it seemed only fitting that I write his story. While this was a fun story to write, it was also a difficult one. I had to really dig deep to understand these characters and why they made some of the life choices they did.

Life would be so much easier if we would travel from point A to point B in a straight line. But that isn't the way it always works, is it? However, God never leaves us no matter how many detours we make. His promise is that He will be with us *always* and He *will* complete what He promised.

Like Ryan and Kait, in *Oklahoma Reunion*, I, too, stand on those promises.

I hope you enjoyed this story. Please let me know by dropping me a line at tina@tinaradcliffe.com or my website, www.tinaradcliffe.com.

Tina Radcliffe

Questions for Discussion

1. In *Oklahoma Reunion,* Ryan mentions God's best for his life. What do you think about this? Does God have a plan for us? What do you think happens when we detour from this plan?

2. A major theme of *Oklahoma Reunion* is promises. Ryan made a promise to Kait with his promise ring. Eight years later he was able to fulfill that promise. Did that synchronicity resonate with you?

3. Another theme of this story is forgiveness. When we ask God to forgive us He does. But how can we handle those around us who refuse to forgive, such as Kait's father?

4. Kait and Ryan both must deal with forgiving themselves and each other. Have you ever dealt with this issue? What is your advice for these characters?

5. Kait struggles with feelings of unworthiness in the eyes of the Jones family, especially Ryan's mother. Have you ever felt this way?

How can she deal with Elizabeth Delaney Jones in love?

6. Ryan wants to recall the past, while Kait struggles to make peace with her past. Is it wise to delve into the past? What are your experiences?

7. What is your favorite scene in *Oklahoma Reunion?* Why?

8. The house Kait returns to belonged to her grandmother and her mother. When she walks into the kitchen, the wonderful memories of those good times past surround her. Can you relate to this? What one memory in particular stands out for you?

9. Another theme of this story is coming home. Can we really go home again? What do you think?

10. *Oklahoma Reunion* is set in the fictional small town of Granby, Oklahoma. Even the mailman knows your name in this town. Are you familiar with small towns like this?

11. Kait mentions "God's timing" and "change" in her dialogue with her daughter. Do you

believe change frightens people? Is God's timing a concept you can relate to?

12. It is human nature to hold back after we have been hurt. Kait is a very brave woman, but she is afraid to be vulnerable and accept Ryan's love. What changes her mind?

13. Ryan is almost too good-natured. He must learn to stand up for Kait and their love. Does he accomplish this?

14. Which characters in *Oklahoma Reunion* were your favorite? Why?

15. Grandpa Jones talks about prayer. Sometimes it seems that prayer is too simplistic an answer for our problems. What do you think? What happens when we pray?

LARGER-PRINT BOOKS!

GET 2 FREE
LARGER-PRINT NOVELS
PLUS 2 FREE
MYSTERY GIFTS

Love Inspired

Larger-print novels are now available...

SUSPENSE

RIVETING INSPIRATIONAL ROMANCE

Watch for our series of edge-
of-your-seat suspense novels.
These contemporary tales
of intrigue and romance
feature Christian characters
facing challenges to their faith...
and their lives!

AVAILABLE IN REGULAR
& LARGER-PRINT FORMATS

For exciting stories that reflect traditional values,
visit:
www.ReaderService.com